"Ladies and gentlemen," the radio announcer said gravely, "the President of the United States!"

"My friends," said a voice familiar to all Americans, "I was informed today that unidentified aircraft have been sighted along the California coast. At this hour we have unconfirmed word of landings by these craft. Various military units have been called out...."

The Three Investigators were stunned by the Presidential broadcast. No nation had been threatening war with the United States. Who could the invaders be?

The boys had no way of knowing. But they never guessed that the invaders might come from outer space!

The Mystery
of the
Blazing Cliffs

by
M. V. Carey

based on characters created by Robert Arthur

BULLSEYE BOOKS

ALFRED A. KNOPF • NEW YORK

Contents

A Word from Hector Sebastian

Welcome, mystery lovers!

I have known the Three Investigators only briefly, but I am mightily impressed by them —and I am delighted to find myself again introducing them to those who aren't already acquainted with their exploits.

Jupiter Jones, First Investigator and leader of the group, is a sturdy boy with a wonderful memory and a talent for finding the truth of the most bizarre situations. Pete Crenshaw, Second Investigator, is loyal, athletic, and often scared witless by the trouble Jupe gets him into. Bob Andrews, the Records and Research man of the team, is a quiet, studious boy who is nonetheless capable of courageous action. All three boys live in the small coastal town of Rocky Beach, California.

As you turn the pages of this book, you will

meet a millionaire who builds a fortress to keep out the world, and a woman who waits to be rescued by heroes from a distant universe. Fantastic? Yes, it is. It's dangerous, too, as the Three Investigators discover when they confront an intergalactic voyager on a mysterious mission to earth.

If I have aroused your interest, I am pleased. Now turn to Chapter 1 and plunge into the adventure.

HECTOR SEBASTIAN

The Mystery
of the
Blazing Cliffs

1

The Angry Man

"Put one finger on that car and I'll horsewhip you!" shouted Charles Barron.

Jupiter Jones stood in the driveway of The Jones Salvage Yard and stared. He wondered if Barron was joking.

But Barron was not joking. His lean body was tense with rage. The face beneath the iron-gray hair was red. He clenched his fists and glared at Hans, one of the two Bavarian brothers who helped out at the yard.

Hans's face was pale with shock. He had just offered to move Mr. Barron's Mercedes, which was blocking the drive in front of the salvage-yard office. "A truck comes in soon with a load of timbers," Hans tried to explain again. "There is no room for it to pass the car. If I move the car—"

"You will not move the car!" roared Barron. "I

3

am sick of incompetents making free with my property! I parked my car in a perfectly good place! Don't you people have any idea how to do business?"

Jupiter's uncle, Titus Jones, appeared suddenly from behind a stack of salvage. "Mr. Barron," he said sternly, "we appreciate your business, but you have no call to abuse my helpers. Now, if you don't want Hans to move your car, you'd better move it yourself. And you'd better hurry because no matter what you decide to do, my truck is coming in!"

Barron opened his mouth as if to shout again, but before he could utter a sound, a slender middle-aged woman with brown hair hurried from the back of the yard. She took hold of his arm and looked at him in a pleading way. "Charles, do move the car," she said. "I'd hate to see anything happen to it."

"I don't intend to have anything happen to it," snapped Barron. He got into the Mercedes and started the engine. An instant later he was maneuvering the car into the empty space next to the office, and the larger of the two salvage-yard trucks was rolling through the gate with a load of scrap lumber.

The brown-haired woman smiled at Hans. "My husband really doesn't mean to be unkind," she said. "He's . . . he's got an impatient nature and . . ."

"I can drive a car," said Hans. "For years I am driving for Mr. Jones and I do not have accidents."

Hans then turned on his heel and walked away.

"Oh, dear!" said Mrs. Barron. She looked helplessly from Uncle Titus to Jupiter and from Jupiter to Aunt Mathilda, who had just come out of the office.

"What's the matter with Hans?" said Aunt Mathilda. "He looks like a walking thunderstorm."

"I'm afraid my husband was rude to him, Mrs. Jones," said Mrs. Barron. "Charles is in a testy mood today. The waitress at breakfast spilled the coffee, and Charles gets so upset when people don't do their jobs well. Nowadays they often don't, you know. Sometimes I wish that the time for deliverance was really here."

"Deliverance?" said Uncle Titus.

"Yes. When the rescuers come from Omega," said Mrs. Barron.

Uncle Titus looked blank. But Jupiter nodded with understanding.

"There's a book called *They Walk Among Us* that tells about the rescuers," Jupiter explained to his uncle. "It's by a man named Contreras. It describes a race of people from the planet Omega. They are keeping watch over us, and eventually, after a catastrophe overwhelms our planet, they'll rescue some of us so that our civilization won't be lost forever."

"Oh, you know about the deliverance!" cried Mrs. Barron. "How nice!"

"Ridicu—" Uncle Titus started to say when Aunt Mathilda spoke up in a brisk, no-nonsense tone. "Jupiter knows about a great many things," she said. "Sometimes I think he knows too much."

Aunt Mathilda then took Mrs. Barron's arm and led her away. She was talking rapidly about the virtues of several used kitchen chairs when Jupe's closest friends, Pete Crenshaw and Bob Andrews, ambled into the salvage yard.

"Morning, Pete," said Uncle Titus. "How are you, Bob? You're just in time. Mrs. Jones has a big job lined up for you boys. She'll tell you about it as soon as we finish with these customers."

Without waiting for an answer, Uncle Titus went off with Mr. Barron, who had locked his car and who now seemed to be angry with the world in general rather than with Hans in particular.

"You missed the excitement," said Jupiter to his friends, "but there may be more."

"What happened?" demanded Bob.

Jupiter grinned. "We've got a bad-tempered customer. But when he isn't yelling at Hans, he's picking out very unusual items to buy." Jupe gestured toward the back of the yard.

Jupiter's uncle and aunt were showing Mr. and Mrs. Barron an old-fashioned treadle sewing machine which was still in working order. As the boys watched, Uncle Titus lifted the machine and carried it toward the other things that Charles Barron had purchased that day. These included two wood-burning stoves, a churn with a broken handle, an ancient hand loom, and a hand-cranked phonograph.

"What a pile of junk!" said Pete. "What are those people going to do with a broken churn? Turn it into a planter?"

"Maybe they collect antiques," guessed Bob.

"I don't think so," said Jupe, "though some of those things *are* old enough to be antiques. But the Barrons seem to want to use everything. Mr. Barron has been questioning Uncle Titus to make sure they can. Some of the things are broken, like the churn, but all of them can be fixed again. The stoves are already in good shape. Mr. Barron took the lids off and looked at the grates to make sure they were intact, and he's buying all the stovepipe we have on hand."

"I'll bet Aunt Mathilda is happy," said Pete. "Now she can unload some of that junk she thought she'd never get rid of. Maybe she'll get lucky and those people will turn into steady customers."

"She'd like that, but Uncle Titus wouldn't," said Jupe. "He can't stand Mr. Barron. The man is rude and unreasonable, and he's been in a rage since he arrived at eight this morning and found the gate still locked. He said it didn't do much good for him to get up before dawn if everyone else in the world slept until noon."

"He said that at eight in the morning?" asked Bob.

Jupe nodded. "Yes, he did. Mrs. Barron seems nice enough, but Mr. Barron is sure that either everyone is trying to cheat him or no one knows his own business."

Bob looked thoughtful. "His name's Barron, huh? There was an article about a man named Barron in the *Los Angeles Times* a few weeks ago. If it's the same man, he's a millionaire who bought a ranch up north somewhere. He's going to grow his own food and be self-sufficient."

"So that's what the churn is all about," said

Pete. "He's going to churn his own butter and . . . and . . . Hey Jupe, he's headed right for Headquarters!"

It was true! At the far side of the yard, Charles Barron had pushed aside a splintery plank so that he could examine a rusted lawn chair. Jupe saw that he was very close to the barrier of carefully arranged salvage that concealed an old mobile-home trailer—a trailer that was the Headquarters of the boys' detective agency, The Three Investigators.

"I'll get him away from there," said Jupe, who did not want to remind Aunt Mathilda that the trailer existed. True, Aunt Mathilda and Uncle Titus had given the mobile home to Jupe and his friends to use for a clubhouse, but they did not know that there was now a telephone in the trailer, a small but efficient laboratory, and a photographic darkroom. They knew that the boys called themselves investigators and had helped solve some mysteries, but they were not really aware of how seriously the boys took the detective business—and how often they found themselves in real danger. Aunt Mathilda would not have approved. She believed in keeping boys busy at safe, practical pursuits such as repairing old items that might be resold in the salvage yard.

Jupiter left his friends standing in the drive and hurried to the side of the yard. Mr. Barron looked around and scowled as he approached, but Jupe pretended not to notice.

"You really appreciate old things," he said to Barron. "We have an old claw-legged bathtub over near the workshop, and a buckboard that looks old, but isn't. It was made for a western movie and it's in perfect condition."

"We don't need a bathtub," said Barron, "but I might have a look at that wagon."

"I'd forgotten about it," said Uncle Titus. "Jupe, thank you for mentioning it."

He and Aunt Mathilda led Barron and his wife away from the Headquarters area, and Jupe returned to his friends.

Jupiter, Pete, and Bob were still loitering near the office when Barron and his wife came back, having decided against the buckboard. They stood in the driveway with Uncle Titus and began to discuss arrangements for having their purchases delivered.

"We're about ten miles north of San Luis Obispo and four miles off the main highway," said Barron. "I can send a man down here with a truck to pick the things up, but I'd prefer not to. My people are busy right now. If you can deliver the stoves and the other things, I'll pay you what it's worth."

He paused and looked suspiciously at Uncle Titus. "I will not pay *more* than it's worth," he added.

"And I wouldn't charge more than it's worth, Mr. Barron," said Uncle Titus. "Just the same, we're not really set up to handle deliveries so far away. . . ."

Mr. Barron began to look angry.

"Just a second, Uncle Titus," interrupted Jupe. His round face was earnest under his shock of dark hair. "You were thinking of going north anyway, remember? To check out that block of old apartment buildings in San Jose, the ones that are scheduled for demolition and that might have some usable salvage. You could drop off Mr. Barron's things on the way, and the delivery wouldn't cost too much."

"Good heavens!" exclaimed Barron. "A young person who can think ahead. Will wonders never cease?"

"Young people are often very intelligent," said Uncle Titus coldly. "All right. That's a good idea. Someone should see that demolition job in San Jose. But that's a two-day trip. I couldn't go for at least a week."

"We could go," said Jupe quickly. "You promised that we'd have a chance to try buying salvage one day soon." Jupe turned to include Pete and Bob in the conversation. "What about it?" he said to them. "Want to go up north?"

"Well, okay," said Pete. "If my folks don't mind."

Bob nodded in agreement.

"Then it's settled!" said Jupiter quickly. "Hans or Konrad can drive the truck for us. We'll stop at Mr. Barron's ranch on the way to San Jose."

Jupe walked away quickly before Charles Barron or Uncle Titus could think of a better plan.

"What's the big idea?" said Pete when the boys were in Jupe's outdoor workshop, safely out of earshot. "We're probably going to have to unload that truck at Barron's place, and that will be one huge job. Since when are you so eager for extra work?"

Jupe leaned against his workbench and grinned. "First of all, Uncle Titus has been promising us a buying trip for a long time, and something has always gotten in the way."

"Yeah, like a sinister scarecrow," said Bob, remembering a buying trip that had recently been canceled by a fiendish apparition in a corn patch. That had been one of the scariest mysteries The Three Investigators had ever solved.

"And second of all," continued Jupe, "it would be a good idea for us to get out of town right now."

Pete gaped. "Why?"

"Because of the really huge job Aunt Mathilda has for us. She wants us to scrape the rust off some old playground equipment and then paint everything. But it's not worth the effort. The metal is too badly rusted. I told her that, but she doesn't believe me. She thinks I'm just trying to get out of work."

"Which you are," said Bob.

"Well, yes," admitted Jupe. "But maybe while we're gone, Hans or Konrad will start the job and Aunt Mathilda will see it isn't worth the time and will sell the playground things for scrap metal.

"And there's a third reason for going north," added Jupe. "The Barrons are a very odd couple, and I'd like to see their place. Do they really have a ranch that's entirely self-sufficient? Do they have only old things, or do they use modern technology, too? And is Mr. Barron always so angry? And Mrs. Barron—does she really believe in the rescuers?"

"Rescuers?" said Pete. "Who are they?"

"A race of superbeings who will rescue us when a great disaster overtakes our planet," said Jupe.

"You're kidding!" said Bob.

"Nope," said Jupe, and his eyes sparkled with glee. "Who knows? Maybe the disaster will hit when we're at the ranch, and we'll get rescued! It could be a very interesting trip!"

2

The Fortress

It was after noon the next day when Hans's brother, Konrad, set out with the larger of the two salvage-yard trucks. Mr. Barron's purchases had been loaded in the back, and Jupiter, Pete, and Bob had wedged themselves in among the old stoves and the other items from Uncle Titus's stock.

"Did you find the newspaper article about Barron?" Jupiter asked Bob as the truck sped north along the Coast Highway.

Bob nodded and took several folded sheets of paper out of his pocket. "It was in the financial section of the *Times* four weeks ago," he reported. "I made a copy of it on the duplicating machine at the library."

He unfolded the papers. "His full name is Charles Emerson Barron," Bob said. "He's a really rich guy. He's always been rich. His father owned Barron International, the company that makes tractors and farm machinery. The Barrons owned Barronsgate, too—the town near Milwaukee where Charles Barron was born. It was an old-time company town, and everybody who lived there worked in the tractor factory and did what the Barrons told them to.

"Mr. Barron inherited Barron International when he was twenty-three, and for a while everything was okay. But then the workers at Barron International went on strike for shorter hours and more money. Eventually Mr. Barron had to give them what they wanted. That made him mad, so he sold the tractor factory and bought a company that made tires. But before long the government fined his tire factory for polluting the air. He sold that and bought a company that had some patents on photographic processes, and he got sued for discriminatory hiring practices. At different times Barron has owned newspapers and a chain of radio stations and some banks, and he has always gotten tangled up in government regulations or labor troubles or lawsuits. So finally he sold everything and moved to a ranch in a valley north of

San Luis Obispo, where he lives in the house he was born in—"

"I thought he was born near Milwaukee," said Pete.

"He was. He had the house moved to California. You can do that sort of thing when you've got heaps of money, and Mr. Barron sure does have heaps. He always made a profit when he sold things. They called him the Robber Barron."

"Of course," said Jupe. "He's just as high-handed as the robber-baron industrialists of the last century. What else could they call him?"

"I suppose they could call him the world's champion grump," said Bob. "According to Barron, savages are taking over the world and nobody takes pride in his work anymore and soon our money won't be worth anything. The only things worth having will be gold and land, and that's why he bought Rancho Valverde. He says he's going to spend the rest of his life on Valverde and raise his own food and experiment with new crops."

Bob put the newspaper article back in his pocket and the boys rode on in silence. The truck sped past small towns and then through open country where the hills were beginning to turn brown under the summer sun.

It was almost three when Konrad turned off the Coast Highway onto State Highway 16SJ, a two-lane road that ran toward the east. In a few moments the truck climbed a short, steep grade. Then the road dipped suddenly into a narrow valley. There were no houses and no other cars.

"This gets to be wild country awfully fast," observed Pete.

"It's going to get wilder still," Jupe told him. "I looked at the map before we left Rocky Beach. There isn't a town between here and the San Joaquin Valley."

The truck rumbled up over more hills, then slowed as it started down a series of hairpin curves. The boys saw that they were headed down into a vast natural bowl, flat at the bottom and bounded with sheer cliffs. The road twisted and doubled back on itself, the engine groaned and complained, and at last they were at the bottom and driving along on flat land. The dark growth of scrub plants crowded the road on the right, and a high chain-link fence edged it on the left. Beyond the fence there was a hedge of oleanders. Occasional breaks in the hedge showed fields where new crops grew in feathery green rows.

"Rancho Valverde," Bob decided.

Konrad drove for more than a mile before he slowed and turned left. The truck passed through an open gate onto a graveled drive that ran north between cultivated fields and citrus groves.

Jupe stood up and looked over the cab of the truck. He saw a large grove of eucalyptus trees ahead, with buildings sheltered under them. To the right of the drive was a sprawling, two-story ranch house which faced south toward the road. To the left and also facing south was an old-fashioned, high-roofed house which was almost a mansion. It was ornate with wooden ginger-bread trim and had towers jutting above the broad, breezy veranda that ran across the front and around the sides.

"I'll bet that's the house Barron moved here from Milwaukee," Bob said.

Jupe nodded. In a moment they had passed between the big house and the simpler ranch house and were driving past a dozen or more small frame cottages, where dark-haired, dark-eyed children played. The children stopped their games to wave at the truck as it went by. There was no sign of an adult until they reached a huge open area at the end of the gravel lane. It was a place where trucks and tractors were parked near large sheds and barns. As Konrad applied the brakes, a red-haired, red-faced man appeared in the doorway of one of the sheds. He had a clipboard in his hands, and he squinted up at Konrad.

"You from The Jones Salvage Yard?" he asked.

Jupe jumped down from the back of the truck. "I am Jupiter Jones," he said importantly. He gestured toward Konrad. "This is Konrad Schmid, and these are my friends, Pete Crenshaw and Bob Andrews."

The red-haired man smiled. "I'm Hank Detweiler," he said. "I'm Mr. Barron's foreman."

"Okay," said Konrad. "Where do you want that we should unload the truck?"

"I don't want," Detweiler said. "Our own people will take care of it."

As if at a signal, three men came out of the shed and began taking things out of the truck. Like the children outside the cottages, these men were dark. They spoke softly in Spanish as they worked, and Hank Detweiler checked off items on a list that was attached to his clipboard. The foreman had blunt, thick hands with the fingernails cut short and square. His face was almost crimson, as if he had a permanent case of windburn, and there were fine lines at the corners of his eyes and around his mouth.

"Well?" he said suddenly, when he glanced up and saw that Jupe was watching him. "Something you wanted to know?"

Jupe smiled. "Well, you could confirm a deduction of mine. Deducing things about people is sort of my hobby," he explained. He looked around at the towering cliffs that enclosed the ranch on three sides, making it a landlocked oasis that was very still and peaceful in the sunny afternoon. "From the way your skin is weathered, I deduce that you haven't been here in this sheltered valley too long," said Jupe. "I think you must be used to wide open spaces and lots of wind."

For an instant there was a sadness in Detweiler's eyes. "Very good," he said. "You're right. I was foreman at the Armstrong Ranch near Austin, Texas, until Mr. Barron came to visit there last year and hired me away. He made me a good offer, but sometimes this place does seem kind of hedged in."

Detweiler put his clipboard down on the hood of a pickup truck that stood near the shed. "You boys come all the way from Rocky Beach to help unload this stuff?" he said. "That's pretty generous of you. Don't know as I'd have done the same when I was your age. But then maybe you're curious about the ranch?"

Jupiter nodded eagerly, and Detweiler grinned.

"Okay," said Detweiler. "If you've got time, I'll show you around. It's an interesting place— not your usual run-of-the-mill truck farm."

The foreman led the way into the shed where the purchases from the salvage yard were being stored. Konrad and the boys saw a warehouse that was crammed to the rafters with all sorts of objects, from machine parts to leather hides to bolts of cloth.

Next door to the warehouse was a smaller building that housed a machine shop. There the visitors were introduced to John Aleman, a snub-nosed young man who was the mechanic for the ranch.

"John keeps our vehicles running and all our machinery in order," said Detweiler. "Course he shouldn't be here. He should be out designing big power plants and irrigation systems."

"Kind of hard to get a job designing a power plant when you quit school after the tenth grade," said Aleman, but he didn't seem unhappy.

Next to the machine shop were sheds used for food storage, and beyond these was a dairy barn which was empty at this hour.

"We have Guernseys here on the ranch," said Detweiler. "Right now the herd is grazing in the pasture up at the north end, under the dam. We have beef cattle, too, and sheep and pigs and chickens. And of course we've got horses."

Detweiler went on to the stable, where a sandy-haired young woman named Mary Sedlack was crouched in a stall next to a handsome palomino stallion. She had the horse's left rear hoof in her hands, and she was frowning at something she saw in the frog of the horse's foot.

"Mary tends to our animals when they get sick," said Detweiler. "Other times she just plain babies them."

"Better stand back," the girl warned. "Asphodel gets nervous if he thinks somebody's crowding him."

"Asphodel is one ornery horse," said Hank Detweiler. "Mary's the only one who can get anywhere near him."

Detweiler and the visitors retreated to the parking area, where they got into a small sedan. Detweiler drove slowly out along a dirt track that ran north through the fields, away from the storage buildings.

"Forty-seven people work here on the ranch," said the foreman. "That's not counting the children, of course, or the people Mr. Barron considers his own personal staff —specialists like Mary and John—and the supervisors. I'm the chief supervisor, and I'm responsible for everything that comes in here or goes out. Then there's Rafael Banales."

Detweiler waved to a thin, not very tall man who stood at the edge of a field where laborers were planting some sort of crop. "Rafe is in charge of the field workers. He is one very progressive farmer. He's a graduate of the University of California at Davis."

They went on, and Detweiler showed them the small building where John Aleman was experimenting with solar energy. He pointed to the slopes under the cliffs to the east, several miles away, where beef cattle grazed. He came at last to a lush green pasture beyond the fields of carrots and lettuce and peppers and squash. The dairy herd was there, and beyond the pasture was a cement dam.

"We have our own water supply for emergencies," Detweiler told Konrad and the boys. "The reservoir beyond that dam is fed by the stream you see falling down the face of that cliff. We haven't had to use that water yet, but it's there if we need it. Right now we use artesian wells. In an emergency we can generate our own power for the pumps, and for all our other electrical needs. Aleman built the generators and they use diesel fuel. If that runs out, we can convert and burn coal or wood."

Detweiler turned the car around and started back toward the cluster of buildings under the eucalyptus trees.

"We keep bees here so we have a source of sugar," he said. "We also have a smokehouse for curing hams and bacon. We have underground storage tanks for our reserve gasoline supply and root cellars for keeping potatoes and turnips. We have miles of shelves to hold the canned things that Elsie and the other women put up when the crops are ripe."

"Elsie?" said Jupiter.

Detweiler grinned. "Elsie is not the least of our specialists," he said. "She cooks for John and Rafael and Mary and me, and for the Barrons, too. If you've got time to stop at the ranch house before you leave, she's sure to spring for some soda pop all around."

Detweiler parked the car near the storage sheds and led Konrad and the boys down the lane toward the ranch house.

Elsie Spratt turned out to be a hearty woman

somewhere in her thirties. She had short blond hair and a broad, easy smile, and she presided over a kitchen that was bright with sunlight and warm with the smell of cooking food. When Hank Detweiler introduced the visitors, she hurried to pour cups of coffee for the men, and she took bottles of soda pop from the refrigerator for the boys.

"Enjoy it while you may," she said cheerily. "Comes the revolution, there won't be any soda pop."

Konrad sat down at the long table beside Detweiler. "Revolution?" he said. "We do not have revolutions in America. If we do not like the President, soon we elect a new one."

"Aha!" said Elsie. "But suppose the system breaks down. What do we do then?"

Konrad looked puzzled, and Jupe glanced around the kitchen. His eyes rested on the wood-burning stove that stood beside the big gas range.

"The system breaks down?" said Jupe. "That's what you're getting ready for here, isn't it? This place is like a fortress—stocked with supplies so that it can go through a siege. It's like one of the castles in the Middle Ages."

"Exactly right," said Detweiler. "What we're doing here is getting ready for the end of the world—or at least for the end of our way of life."

Elsie poured a cup of coffee for herself. As she sat down and took a spoonful of sugar, Jupe noticed that there was a slight deformity on her right hand—a jutting bit of bone and flesh on her smallest finger.

"I don't think we're getting ready for the kind of revolution where we drag the President out and shoot him," she said. "I think what Mr. Barron has in mind is a time when everything sort of falls apart and we have famine and looting and confusion and bloodshed. You know. He thinks the world is *really* going to the dogs, and we have to be prepared if we're going to survive."

"Mr. Barron believes that gold and land are the only safe investments, doesn't he?" said Jupiter. "Obviously he expects a collapse of the prevailing monetary system."

Elsie Spratt stared at him. "Do you always talk that way?" she asked.

Pete chuckled. "Jupe doesn't believe in using short words if long ones will do as well."

Jupe ignored this jibe. "Do *you* think our world is coming to an end?" he asked Elsie and Detweiler.

Elsie shrugged. "No, I suppose not."

"I think Mr. Barron's the only one who really believes it," said Detweiler. "He claims the government is poking its nose into places where it doesn't belong, and people nowadays don't have to work if they don't want to, and so most people don't. He says that sooner or later our money won't be worth anything—"

"Shhh!" said Elsie.

She put a hand on Detweiler's arm and looked past him to the door. Mrs. Barron stood there on the other side of the screen. "May I come in?" she said.

"Of course." Elsie got up. "We were just having coffee. Would you like a cup?"

"No, thank you." Mrs. Barron stepped into the kitchen and smiled at Jupiter, Pete, and Bob. "I saw you boys come in," she said. "I wonder if you could stay a bit longer and have dinner with Mr. Barron and myself?"

Konrad scowled. "Jupe, it is after five," he said. "We should go now."

Mrs. Barron turned to Elsie. "We could eat early, couldn't we?" she said.

Elsie looked startled. "I guess so."

"There now!" Mrs. Barron smiled again, and Jupe looked questioningly at Bob and then at Pete.

"That would be swell," said Pete.

"Don't worry," said Bob to Konrad. "We'll get to San Jose sooner or later."

"Then it's settled," said Mrs. Barron. "We'll sit down at five-thirty."

She went out and down the back steps of the ranch house.

"I do not like this," said Konrad. "I think we should go."

"In a little while, Konrad," said Jupe. "Another hour or so won't make any difference."

Jupiter's deductions and predictions were usually right. But this time he couldn't have been more wrong.

3

No Exit

"Mrs. Barron likes boys," said Hank Detweiler. "She has two adopted sons and she misses them. One went off to be a drummer with a rock group, and the other lives in Big Sur now and makes wooden clogs that he sells to tourists. He writes poetry, too."

"Gee," said Pete. "How does Mr. Barron feel about that?"

"Not a bit happy," said Elsie Spratt. "You boys go along and have your dinner and be nice to Mrs. Barron, but watch out for him. When he's in a bad mood, he's cozy as a rattlesnake in a rainstorm."

Konrad looked upset. "I think I will not go," he announced. "I will stay here and wait." He glanced at Elsie. "It is okay if I stay here?" he asked.

"Why, sure," said Elsie. "You can have your

dinner here while the boys are living it up over in the big house."

And so Jupiter, Pete, and Bob left the ranch house at five-thirty and walked across the drive to the Barron house. Mrs. Barron opened the door for them and then led them into a parlor that was stiffly formal, with settees and chairs upholstered in velvet. Mr. Barron was there, complaining loudly that there was something wrong with the television set. "Nothing but noise and snow!" he said. He shook hands with the boys in an absent-minded way. "You young fellows are in school, I suppose," he said. "Learning anything? Or are you just putting in your time?"

Before the boys could answer, a Mexican woman came to the doorway to announce that dinner was served. Mr. Barron offered his arm to Mrs. Barron, and the boys followed them to the dining room.

The Mexican woman had brought the dinner across from Elsie's kitchen, and it was delicious. Jupe ate slowly and listened to Mr. Barron's lecture on the evils of plastic in almost any form. He learned that Mr. Barron did not approve of vinyl that masqueraded as leather, or of polyester that pretended to be wool. Mr. Barron also took time to condemn termite inspectors who did not understand termites and auto mechanics who could not fix cars properly.

Mrs. Barron waited until her husband had finished his list of grievances. Then she began to talk quietly about her son in Big Sur who wrote poetry.

"Trash!" snapped Mr. Barron. "The stuff doesn't even rhyme! That's the trouble with the world today. Poetry doesn't rhyme and people don't have to work to earn a living and children don't have to respect their parents and—"

"Charles, dear, I think you have a crumb on your chin," said Mrs. Barron.

Mr. Barron dabbed at himself with a napkin, and Mrs. Barron told the boys about her other son who played drums for a musical group.

"He's going to be here in August," said Mrs. Barron, "for the convention."

Mr. Barron made a choking sound, and his face grew very red. "Mob of zanies!" he grumbled.

"Convention?" said Pete timidly.

"The annual meeting of the Blue Light Mission will take place here in August," said Mrs. Barron. She smiled at Jupiter. "You know about that—you've read the book. So many members of our society have talked with the rescuers who come from the planet Omega. They'll share their experiences with the rest of us, and if we're lucky we'll have Vladimir Contreras for our speaker this year."

"Oh, yes," said Jupe. "The man who wrote *They Walk Among Us.*"

Mr. Barron leaned back in his chair. "Last year the convention of the Blue Light Mission was held in a cornfield in Iowa and a man came who believed that the earth is hollow and that a race of superbeings live inside it," he said. "There was also a woman who told fortunes with magnetized needles that floated on water, and a pimply youth who kept saying 'Om! Om!' until I wanted to hit him."

"*You* went to the convention?" said Pete to Barron.

"I had to!" snapped Barron. "My wife is a remarkable woman, but if I left her to herself, she would surely be victimized by those loonies. Even when I am with her, she becomes overenthusiastic. I was unable to keep her from inviting that weird group here this summer."

"We should have a large turnout," said Mrs. Barron happily. "Many people are keenly interested. They know that the rescuers are out there watching us."

"The only ones who are out there watching us are anarchists and criminals who want to take over," said Mr. Barron. "Well, I'm ready for them!"

Pete looked pleadingly at Jupe, who stood up.

"It was very kind of you to invite us," said Jupe, "but we must go. Konrad is anxious to get to San Jose."

"Of course," said Mrs. Barron. "We mustn't make you late."

She walked to the door with the boys, and she stood and watched them go down the front steps.

"You have a good time?" asked Elsie Spratt when they came into the ranch-house kitchen.

"Interesting," said Bob, "but not cozy. You said it."

Elsie laughed. "A rattlesnake in a rainstorm."

Konrad had just finished his dinner. He carried his dishes to the sink, and then the four visitors went out to the truck. Detweiler stood on the porch of the ranch house as they drove out, waving good-bye to them.

"Nice people," said Bob.

"Except for Mr. Barron," said Pete. "What a grump!"

The truck rumbled down the lane, and when it neared the gate a mile away it slowed. Then it stopped and the boys heard Konrad open the door of the cab.

"Jupe?" Konrad called.

Jupe jumped down from the back of the truck, followed by his friends. They saw a man standing in the road, blocking the way. The man wore an army uniform, and there were cartridges in the belt at his waist. A helmet was buckled under his chin. He held a rifle at the ready across his chest.

"Sorry," he said. "The road is closed."

"What's the trouble?" said Jupiter.

"I don't know," said the soldier. His voice shook as if he were afraid. "I've got orders that no one gets past. The road is closed."

He shifted the rifle slightly, as if to draw attention to it. It slipped in his grasp and began to fall.

"Watch it!" yelled Pete.

The soldier grabbed clumsily at the gun, and with a stunning roar it went off!

4

Invasion!

The sound of the explosion echoed through the valley. The young soldier stared at his gun, shocked, his eyes enormous in his pale face.

"That thing is loaded!" said Konrad, outraged.

"It sure is," said the soldier shakily. "We were issued live ammunition today."

He gripped the rifle more firmly, fearful that it might slip and go off again. The boys heard the sound of a car on the road. An instant later a jeep came speeding into sight. It stopped just feet from the armed man.

"Stanford, what do you think you're doing?" demanded the officer who sat in the jeep next to the driver. He glared at the soldier, then at the boys and Konrad.

"Sorry, sir," said the soldier. "The gun slipped."

"Stanford, if you can't hold on to a rifle, you don't belong out here," said the officer.

"No, sir," said the soldier.

The officer got out of the jeep and stalked toward Konrad. The boys saw that he was young—as young as the frightened soldier. His olive-drab field jacket was new. So was his helmet. So were the expensive-looking combat boots on his feet.

"I'm Lieutenant John Ferrante," he said. One gloved hand swung up as if to salute, but then it dropped again. Jupe saw that he was trying to be very military, like an actor portraying an officer in a war film.

"Why is the road closed?" said Konrad. "We are supposed to go to San Jose tonight. We do not have time for the war games that you play."

"Sorry, but it isn't a game." Lieutenant Ferrante's voice was tight. "My men and I were dispatched from Camp Roberts this afternoon and told to keep all traffic off this road. This is an emergency route from the San Joaquin Valley to the coast, and it has to be clear for military vehicles."

"We don't plan to block it," Jupe pointed out. "We're going back to 101, and then north to San Jose."

"Highway 101 is closed, too," said the lieutenant. "Look, why don't you just turn around and go back up that drive and let us do our job?"

The lieutenant put a hand on the pistol he wore at his belt. The boys stiffened.

"I have orders that no one is to use this road," the lieutenant continued. "It's for your own protection."

"Protection?" echoed Konrad. "You protect us with a gun?"

"I'm sorry," said the lieutenant. "Look, I just can't let you through. And I can't tell you any more than I have because I don't know much more. Now be good guys and go back up the drive, huh?"

"Mr. Barron won't believe this," said Jupiter. "That's Charles Emerson Barron, the industrialist. He may be quite angry when he learns that his guests are being detained. He might even call Washington. He's a powerful man, you know!"

"I can't help that," said the lieutenant. "I can't let you through!"

Several more uniformed figures appeared on the road. They stood quietly near the soldier who had first stopped the truck. Each carried a rifle, and the boys could see that each was alert.

"Okay, okay!" said Konrad quickly. "Jupe, I do not like this. We go back to the ranch. We tell Mr. Barron what happens."

"Good!" said the lieutenant. "You do that. And listen—I'll follow you in the jeep. I'll help you explain to this Barron, whoever he is. I mean, it's just one of those things. We're only following orders."

The lieutenant got into his jeep and the boys climbed up into the truck.

"Crazy!" said Pete as Konrad turned on the gravel drive.

"Yes, it is," said Jupiter.

The truck began to roll toward the Barron house, followed by the jeep.

"There was absolutely nothing wrong when we left Rocky Beach at noon," said Jupe. "What could have happened since then?"

"Beats me," said Pete, "but that lieutenant sure looked scared. Something's up."

Konrad stopped the truck in the drive beyond the ranch house. The jeep pulled in behind, and the lieutenant got out and looked around.

"Who's in charge here?" he demanded. His voice was loud, as if he were blustering to keep up his courage.

Hank Detweiler came down the back steps of the ranch house. Elsie Spratt and Mary Sedlack were with him, and Rafael Banales stood behind them in the kitchen doorway and watched.

"I'm Mr. Barron's foreman," said Detweiler. "Can I help you?"

The back door of the Barron house opened and Charles Barron and his wife came out onto the back porch.

"What is it?" asked Barron.

"The road is closed," said Jupiter. "We can't leave."

Jupe turned expectantly toward the lieutenant, and Barron glared at the officer. "My road? Closed?"

Jupe saw with amusement that the lieutenant had begun to sweat in spite of the chill on the evening breeze. Jupe suspected that Charles Emerson Barron often had this effect on people.

"I beg your pardon, sir," said the lieutenant. "It's not y-y-your road!"

Jupe grinned to himself. Mr. Barron could do more than make people sweat. He could also make them stutter.

"Well, it certainly isn't *your* road!" cried Barron. "What do you mean, it's closed? It can't be closed! It's a public highway."

"Y-y-yes, sir!" said the lieutenant. "The highway to the San Joaquin, sir, b-b-but—"

"For heaven's sake, speak up!" roared Barron. "Don't stand there blithering!"

"We h-h-have orders, sir," the lieutenant managed to get out. "This afternoon. From Washington. Something h-h-happened in T-t—"

"Lieutenant!" shouted Barron.

"In Texas!" cried the lieutenant. "S-something happened in Texas." Having gotten a grip on his speech, he took off his helmet and ran one gloved hand over his dark hair. "I don't know what it was, but all roads in the state have been closed—all main arteries, sir. No traffic is moving."

"This is preposterous!" shouted Barron.

"Yes, sir," said the lieutenant.

"I'm going to call Washington," said Barron.

"Yes, sir," said the lieutenant.

"The President," Barron announced. "I'll call the President."

Barron stamped into his house. The windows of the big house were open, and the group gathered on the drive could hear Charles Barron dialing the telephone. There was silence for a second, then Barron jiggled the instrument.

"Blast!" he said.

He slammed out onto the back porch and down the steps. "Dratted phone's dead!" he exclaimed. "Must be a line down!"

"No, sir," said Lieutenant Ferrante. "I don't think so, sir."

"What do you mean?" Barron demanded. "What do you know about this?"

"Nothing, sir," said the lieutenant, "except that telephones aren't working anywhere in the area. Or radios. No radios, sir. Our orders came by wire from Washington."

"No telephones?" demanded Barron. "No radios?"

Men and women began to drift down the lane from the cottages. They were the people who worked for Barron. They seemed frightened as they gathered in the fading light.

"It is true what he says," said one man. "The radio, it does not work."

"We do not have television tonight," said another. "There was nothing on the television but a strange noise. Now there is not even that. The electricity is gone."

"No television?" said Barron. There was an expression that was half fear and half exultation on his face. "No electricity?"

Elsie Spratt made an impatient noise. "This is a scene out of a bad movie," she said. Her voice was loud and determinedly cheerful. "Why would the roads be closed? That doesn't make sense! Exactly what did it say in that wire from Washington? What happened in Texas?"

"I don't know, ma'am," said the lieutenant. "I wasn't told. I just have—"

"I know, I know!" said Elsie. "You have your orders!"

She turned and went noisily up the steps of the ranch house into the big kitchen. Through the open windows the boys saw her twist the knobs on the battery-operated radio that stood on the counter. Almost immediately the sound of music floated out to the people in the drive.

"Hah!" said Elsie. "No radio, huh?"

"One second!" said Jupe. "That music! It's—"

" 'Hail to the Chief'!" said Barron. "It's the piece the Marine Band plays when the President appears!"

The music ended, and there was a moment of silence. Then came the sound of someone clearing his throat.

"Ladies and gentlemen," said an announcer, "the President of the United States!"

Mrs. Barron moved close to her husband. He put his arm around her.

"My friends," said a familiar voice, "I was

informed shortly after noon today that unidentified aircraft have been sighted in parts of Texas
and New Mexico and along the California coast.
At this hour we have word—unconfirmed
word—of landings by these craft in Fort Worth,
Dallas, Taos, and San Francisco. I repeat, these
reports are not confirmed.

"Let me assure you that there is no cause for
alarm. Although communications in parts of the
West seem to be momentarily disrupted, we
have been in touch with the Kremlin and with
other capitals in Europe and South America.
Our relations with governments to the east and
to the south have never been closer, and there
is no cause for alarm. . . ."

"You already said that, you dolt!" snapped
Barron.

"Various military units have been called out,"
the voice went on, "and we ask that all citizens
cooperate with these units by remaining in their
homes so that strategic surface routes will not
be obstructed. Please keep tuned to your local
civil defense—"

There was a mighty blast of static, and Elsie
Spratt's radio went dead.

"Idiot!" said Charles Barron. "Infernal idiot!
How he ever got elected! On the radio for ten

minutes and he told us nothing! Absolutely nothing!"

"Mr. Barron, he as good as told us we're being invaded," said Hank Detweiler. The foreman looked stunned. "An invasion! By someone who has cut our communication lines! We're . . . we're alone here! We can't reach anybody to find out what's going on outside!"

5

"Get Off My Land!"

"Communists!" shouted Charles Barron. "Anarchists! Riffraff! I don't believe there were any aircraft! They've grabbed the radio stations; that's what they've done! They're trying to frighten us into surrender! Or they've taken the President prisoner, or . . . or . . ."

Barron paused. A look of steely determination came over his face. "I'm going to drive into town," he announced. "Better yet, I'll go to Camp Roberts. I'm going to talk to someone who knows what's going on, and no one had better try to stop me!"

"I have orders, sir," said the lieutenant. "N-n-no v-vehicles on the road."

The lieutenant straightened himself, took a deep breath, and spoke slowly and carefully. "I'd appreciate it, Mr. Barron, if you'd remain at the ranch for the time being. My orders, sir, are to keep the road open to the San Joaquin Valley, and to see to the safety of personnel, equipment, and installations at Rancho Valverde."

"Safety?" It was Elsie Spratt who spoke now. She had come out of the kitchen. "Our safety? Why? Who's threatening *us?* What's going on out there, Lieutenant?"

Elsie gestured toward the cliffs—and the world beyond. "What does it have to do with us?" she wanted to know.

"I . . . I don't know, ma'am," said Ferrante.

"Exactly what did your superiors tell you, Lieutenant?" demanded Charles Barron.

The lieutenant did not answer.

"Come, come!" snapped Barron. "What did your commanding officer say to you today?"

Again the lieutenant did not reply.

"It isn't the road they're so worried about, is it?" said Barron. "There are dozens of other roads much more important. It's Rancho Valverde that the people at Camp Roberts want to guard, isn't it? Why? What are we? Some kind of natural resource?"

"Maybe that's just what we are, Mr. Barron," said Elsie Spratt. "I mean, how many places are there in this country that are as . . . as self-sufficient as we are? We can live here for years without going outside!"

"Aha!" cried Barron. "So that's it!"

"What, Charles?" asked Mrs. Barron.

"It's happening," said Barron. "I said it would! All this folderol about unidentified aircraft is a bunch of nonsense to throw us off guard. They want to make everyone stay at home until the top dogs are safe—safe here in my valley!"

"Mr. Barron, I don't understand what—" began Hank Detweiler.

"Understand?" said Barron. "Of course you understand. Either we're being attacked by some foreign power—and you can take your pick which one it might be—or there's been an uprising in the country and it's spreading. Probably started right there in Washington. I read that there was going to be a rally there by some group of people calling themselves Workers United. What are they united *for*, I'd like to know! Sounded like they were up to no good. All they need is a few members in major cities—just a small number of militants—and they can pull down the government in a day!"

"They would have had to do it in less time than that," said Jupiter mildly. "Everything was

normal when we left Rocky Beach this afternoon."

"Things are not normal now," said Barron.
"Something disastrous is going on and that
mediocrity who calls himself a President hasn't
the faintest idea how to deal with it, so he'll run
away! He'll run to a place where he can be safe
and he'll dig in and—"

"Mr. Barron," cried Elsie, "I can't manage if
he's coming here. I was hired to cook for you
and Mrs. Barron and Hank and the others, but
the kitchen isn't big enough for too many more
and—"

"Elsie, you will not be asked to cook for any
of that gang from the East," declared Charles
Barron. "I prepared this retreat so that I would
have a place to live while our civilization
is . . . is adjusting itself. I have a right to enjoy
this property without the presence of government officials of any stripe!"

Barron glared at Lieutenant Ferrante. "You
get off my land," he said. "I have guns and I'm
going to post guards along the perimeter of the
ranch. Trespassers will be shot, do you understand?"

"Yes, sir," said the lieutenant. He climbed
into the jeep. "Move it!" he said to the driver.
"Come on! Let's go!"

A moment later the jeep was speeding off down the lane.

"Hank," said Mr. Barron, "pick ten of the most trustworthy men—men who can shoot——and send them in to see me. We'll have the fence patrolled all along the road."

"But Charles, will that help?" said Mrs. Barron. "If the President does come here, won't he come by helicopter? If the guards are on the road—"

"Be still, Ernestine!" snapped Barron. "You don't understand about these things."

Barron started up the steps to his house, then paused and looked back at the Three Investigators. "You boys," he said. "You can stay here. You're innocent victims, and I won't put you out on the road where idiots like that lieutenant might—well, God knows what he might do. Elsie, would you mind feeding four more?"

"No, Mr. Barron," said the cook.

"Good enough," said Barron, and he went into the house.

Jupiter, Pete, and Bob stood near the truck with Konrad. They watched Hank Detweiler call the names of ten of the ranch workers. The men went one by one up the steps into the Barron house.

By the time the men came out again, it was getting dark, but the boys could see that each man carried a rifle and wore an ammunition belt. They went off down the lane toward the fence and the gate.

Other residents of the ranch drifted away, and when Hank Detweiler emerged from the Barron house, only Konrad and the boys remained in the driveway.

"I don't know what this is all about," said Detweiler, "but I'm sure it will blow over before long. You'll probably be on your way again tomorrow."

He went into the ranch house, which was now lighted by the soft glow of kerosene lamps. After a moment Konrad announced that he would go in, too.

"Well?" said Bob to Jupiter, after Konrad had gone.

"I don't know what to think," said Jupe. "When we left Rocky Beach at noon, everything was fine. Now, only a few hours later, we have no electricity, the radios don't work, and the telephone is dead. The President has made a speech about strange aircraft landing in several parts of the country, and there are soldiers patrolling the road so that we can't drive away."

"Maybe we can't drive away, but we can walk away," said Pete. "If we can get to someplace that's outside—"

He stopped short. "Hey," he said. "I'm beginning to sound like I really believe this place is a fortress—like the rest of the world is outside. We're inside, where it's safe."

"We aren't even sure it's safe," said Jupe. "But you're right. We should walk out to the nearest town. We won't learn anything by staying here. Maybe there really is some sort of invasion going on and we can get more news about it outside."

"But Mr. Barron has guards watching the fence," said Bob. "Will they let us pass?"

"They won't know we're going," said Jupe. "We've gotten past guards before. We can do it again."

"What about the soldiers?" asked Pete.

"We can keep out of their way easily enough," Jupe declared. "They'll probably be watching the gate anyway."

"Okay," said Bob. "Anything's better than just sitting here waiting for the sky to fall."

"Then let's go," said Jupe. "Something strange is going on. I want to know what it is!"

6
The Blazing Cliffs

The Three Investigators slipped quietly down the lane in the darkness.

"I can't see a thing," Pete complained. "It's black as pitch."

"It won't be for long," Jupe predicted.

Even as he spoke, the moon crept up from behind the eastern cliffs. A faint silvery light touched the valley, and the gravel lane suddenly appeared gray-white. In the citrus groves to one side there were shadows under the trees—deep black shadows, sharply etched on the ground.

"Everyone off the drive!" ordered Jupe. "Someone could see us out here." He led the way to the shadows under the orange trees. The three boys went on silently toward the southern boundary of the ranch, where the fence enclosed the property.

Fifteen minutes later they saw the fence, gray-white in the moonlight beyond the dark hedge of oleanders. The boys crept up to the hedge, and standing in the shadows of the bushes, they cautiously looked over them. Now they could see the road beyond the hedge, and the dark undergrowth of the wilderness on the other side of the road. They watched, and they waited.

For a minute or two nothing moved on the road. But then there were headlights. A jeep came along slowly. A searchlight was mounted on the jeep, and the boys had to duck to avoid the beam that swept across the hedge and then swung to the south to probe the wilderness there.

As the jeep passed, a beam of light flashed from the cliffs far to the west of the gate. It danced along the edge of Barron's property.

"Someone's up there watching the fence," said Bob.

Jupiter sighed. "Probably one of Barron's men."

"He might spot us if we try to go over the fence," Pete observed, "and there's a guard near the gate. I can see him from here."

The jeep turned and came back past the gate. It stopped in the road near the spot where the boys waited. Again the watcher on the hillside sent his light stabbing through the night. It rested. on the men in the jeep. There were three of them. One looked up toward the cliff, then took his rifle from his shoulder and checked it, as if to be sure it was loaded. After a moment the jeep rolled on. It topped a small rise and then dipped out of sight in the hollow beyond it.

"Why would Barron's men stop us if we go over the fence?" Bob asked reasonably. "Why would they bother? Doesn't Mr. Barron just want to keep people from coming in?"

"Probably," said Jupiter, "but if Barron's guards see us, they might make some noise that would attract the attention of the soldiers."

"Well, would *they* care?" said Bob. "We're just pedestrians. We wouldn't get in the way of any military vehicles on the road."

"But suppose it isn't really military vehicles the lieutenant is concerned about," Jupe countered. "Suppose what he really wants is to keep the staff of Rancho Valverde bottled up?"

"You sound like Mr. Barron," said Pete, "and I think he's *nuts!*"

"Perhaps he is, but I feel he's right about one thing," said Jupe. "The lieutenant's main interest is the ranch, not the road. He'd probably keep us from leaving. But if we can get across the road into that wilderness area, we could get away."

"Hold it!" cried Pete. "We're only a few miles from the main highway, but if it's a few miles of scrub brush, you can count me out! We'd be cut to ribbons in the dark!"

"You're probably right," said Jupe. "Okay. When I looked at the map before we left Rocky Beach, I saw another road. It's to the north of the ranch. If we could climb the cliffs, we could get to it easily."

Pete turned and stared at the nearest line of cliffs, to the west. The moon was high now, and the cliffs looked bleak as they loomed up in the ghostly light. There were black shadows in places where gullies and ravines broke the surface.

"Okay," said Pete. "We can go out over the cliffs. But not at night, Jupe. Not without a flashlight. It's too steep and the light's too tricky. One mistake there could be our last."

"True," said Jupiter. "All right. Let's go back to the ranch, get some rest, then start out at first light."

The boys began to walk back through the citrus groves toward the ranch house. It was easier going now, with the moonlight and the lamps in the houses ahead to show them their path. When they were a hundred yards or so from the Barron house they got back onto the lane.

"Jupe?" Konrad came around the corner of the ranch house. "Jupe, are you there?" he called. "Pete? Bob?"

"We're here, Konrad," said Jupe.

"Why did you not come into the house?" asked Konrad. "Where did you go? I have been looking for you."

The back door of the Barron house opened and Charles Barron came out. "Who's wandering around out here?" he called.

"It's only us, Mr. Barron," said Pete.

And then he saw a sudden, dazzling blue-white flare of light behind Konrad.

"Jupe!" cried Pete. "Look!"

The cliffs to the north of the ranch were enveloped in strange blue flames! The eerie fire leaped skyward like sheets of cold brilliance.

"What on earth?" cried Charles Barron.

For an instant the fire almost hid the bare granite surface of the cliffs. Then dense billows of white smoke gushed from the land beyond the reservoir.

Doors slammed. Feet pounded on the road. There were cries of wonder and of fear. Then, from out of the billowing, gleaming cloud on the land, an oval-shaped object rose. It hovered in the air, silver in the light from the blazing cliffs. Then it lifted upward. In seconds it was above the cliffs, vanishing into the night sky.

The blaze on the cliffs dwindled and died. There was silence at the ranch—a frozen moment when no one dared to move. Then, "Holy cow!" said Pete. "A flying saucer!"

7

An Innocent Victim

"Preposterous!" said Charles Barron.

No one answered him.

Mrs. Barron came out of the house and down the steps. "Charles!" she said excitedly. "Did you see it?"

"I'm not blind," said Barron. "Whatever it was, I saw it. Hank! Rafael! John!"

Barron pointed toward the northern cliffs. "We're going to see what in tarnation is going on!" he announced.

Jupe heard the roar of a car engine on the road. He turned to see the soldiers' jeep spurting up the lane. It stopped with a lurch just short of the ranch house.

"Mr. Barron?" Lieutenant Ferrante leaped from the vehicle and started toward the ranch owner. "Are you all right?" he said. "What happened? We saw the fire!"

"I will keep you informed of all developments that concern you," snapped Barron. "In the meantime, take yourself and your jeep off my property."

"Charles!" exclaimed Mrs. Barron. "Really! You needn't be so rude!"

"I'll be as rude as I choose, Ernestine," said Barron. "Lieutenant, I'm waiting."

Ferrante climbed back into the jeep. The driver threw the engine into reverse and the jeep backed away from the people who had gathered on the drive. It made a tight turn and sped down the lane.

"Pablito!" said Barron. He beckoned to a thin boy who had been watching the scene.

"Yes, Mr. Barron?" said the boy. He appeared to be eight or nine years old.

"Go down to the fence and find your father and tell him that the guards are to shoot the tires of that jeep if the soldiers try to bring it through the gate again."

Immediately one of the women spoke up. "Pablito will not go with such a message," she said. "If there must be such a message, I will go."

"Charles, all of this hardly seems necessary," said Mrs. Barron. "That poor young man with the jeep is only trying to do his job."

"He's trespassing and I will not put up with trespassers, whatever their age, status, or government affiliation," announced Charles Barron. "We had better get that clear immediately or we'll be up to our hips in refugees and parasites."

Barron turned again to Detweiler. "Hank, you and Rafael and John and I will go to the upper meadow and see what in the name of fury has been going on there."

"Yes, Mr. Barron," said Detweiler. The foreman looked puzzled and curious, but not at all frightened.

"I think we should be armed," said Barron. He took a key ring from his pocket and handed it to Banales, who had come out of the ranch house. "You know where the guns are," he said. "Get a rifle for each of us, and make sure they're loaded."

"Charles, you won't shoot anyone, will you?" said Mrs. Barron.

"Not unless I have to," her husband answered.

Unseen by any of the adults, Jupe tugged at Pete's sleeve and beckoned to Bob. The three boys slipped back through the crowd on the lane and took shelter in the darkness between two of the cottages.

"If we want to know what really happened up there, we'd better beat Barron and the others up to the reservoir," Jupe told his friends. "Barron might just decide to keep the facts to himself."

Pete gulped. "Jupe, those guys have rifles."

"Barron just promised not to shoot anyone," said Jupe, stretching the truth. He trotted off in the direction of the parking area near the sheds.

"But Jupe," pleaded Pete, running after him, "we just saw a flying saucer! There might be aliens up by the dam!"

"All the more reason for us to get there first!" said Jupe.

Pete groaned but followed along with Bob.

It was dark in the shadows near the sheds, but once the boys started across the fields to the north of the parking area, they moved swiftly. In the moonlight they could see the dam, and when they came to the edge of the pasture between the cultivated fields and the dam, they saw sheep grazing. Several bleated in protest as the boys passed. Pete jumped in fright at the sound, but he kept going. Soon the boys were scrambling over the rocks at one side of the dam.

That afternoon Hank Detweiler had mentioned there was a meadow beyond the dam, although he had not actually showed it to them. He believed that the valley containing Rancho Valverde had once been a lake bed. In some long ago age a great earthquake had torn the lake bed in two and lifted the northernmost section above the level of the rest of the valley. Part of this upper level was now covered by the reservoir, and the rest was a meadow that sloped up away from the reservoir to the base of the cliffs.

When the boys reached the top of the dam, they followed a path around the reservoir to the grassy land on the far side of the water. Pete looked fearfully around. Were there aliens up here? He could see no one but his friends. And there was no trace of the fire that had blazed on the cliffs. In the moonlight the boys saw only naked rocks and the grass that made a dark silver carpet between the reservoir and the cliffs.

"We should have brought a light," said Bob. He started through the knee-high grass, but before he had gone many feet he stumbled and almost fell.

"Careful!" warned Jupe.

Bob took a step backward. "Jupe!" he said.

"Pete! Hey! There's something . . . something here!"

Jupe and Pete hurried to his side and knelt in the grass.

"Oh, no!" exclaimed Pete. "A body! Is he . . . is he alive?"

Jupe leaned close to the still body of a man. "Yes. He's still breathing."

There was the sound of voices near the dam, and the clatter of dislodged stones rolling down an incline. Charles Barron and his men were coming.

Jupe gave a mighty heave and the man on the meadow rolled over onto his back. His face showed white in the moonlight. The eyes were closed and the mouth was partly open. His breath came in quick gasps.

There was a faint odor now. It was the smell of singed hair.

"All right!" Charles Barron shouted. "Hold it right there! One move and I'll blow your head off!"

The boys blinked in the glare of flashlights.

"Why, it's the boys from the salvage yard," said Barron.

"Mr. Barron, this man is hurt," Jupiter called.

Barron and Hank Detweiler hurried forward.

"De Luca!" exclaimed Barron. "Simon de Luca!"

Detweiler knelt and held his flashlight close to the man's face. He touched de Luca cautiously.

"He's got a lump right behind the ear," said Detweiler, "and . . . and some of his hair's burned off!"

The unconscious man stirred.

"Okay, Simon," said Detweiler. "We're with you."

The man opened his eyes and stared up at Detweiler.

"What happened?" asked Detweiler.

De Luca moved his head, then winced. "Did I fall?" he asked. He looked around slowly. "The sheep! Where are the sheep?"

"In the lower field, the other side of the dam," said Detweiler.

De Luca sat up carefully. "I don't understand," he said. "I came out to check on the sheep. I came almost to the dam. Everything was okay."

He looked anxiously at Detweiler. "I was in the lower meadow," he said. "That's the last thing I remember. How did I get here? Did you bring me?"

"No, we didn't, Simon," said Detweiler.

"These boys found you here. Do you remember seeing anything? Flames? Smoke? Anything at all?"

"Nothing," said de Luca. He put his head in his hands, and for the first time he touched his hair. "What's happened?" he cried. "My hair! What is the matter with my hair?"

"Simon, you got kind of singed," said Detweiler.

Banales knelt beside the injured man and began to talk softly in Spanish. The others spread out to search the meadow. The light of their torches showed them charred places on the ground, as if flames had burned fiercely and briefly in the green grass. There were sooty streaks on the cliffs where the blue fires had blazed. That was all, except for an object that Detweiler found near the base of the cliffs—a thing no bigger than a man's hand. It was made of lustrous silver-gray metal, and it was hinged in the middle. At either end was a series of prongs.

"Some kind of clamp," said Detweiler. "John, do you know what it is?"

John Aleman took the object from Detweiler and turned it this way and that in his hands. "Beats me," he said. "Looks like it's off some sort of machine."

"Or an aircraft?" asked Detweiler.

"Maybe," said Aleman. "The metal—it's some kind of alloy. I don't know just what. It doesn't look like steel. It's more like pewter. And there's no residue of oil on it. Look. You close it like this and the prongs lock. It could be some sort of switch, but it's not like any switches that I've ever seen."

Barron glared around the meadow and then looked up at the cliffs. "Not like any you've seen?" he said.

They were silent then, thinking of the blazing cliffs and the clouds of smoke, and of the strange craft that had lifted from the meadow. De Luca felt his singed hair. His face was bewildered.

"Someone was here," said Aleman quietly. His square, blunt-featured face was grim. "Somebody came and . . . and did something to Simon and went away again. But where did they come from? And where did they go? Who were they?"

No one answered. From the hills above them came the lonely cry of a coyote. Pete shivered at the wailing sound, and at the memory of the flying saucer. He wondered if aliens had walked in the meadow—if aliens were hiding there right now.

8

Attack!

Simon de Luca was brought back from the meadow by truck. After he was carried into one of the cottages on the lane, Mary Sedlack and Mrs. Barron examined him. They tested his reflexes, peered into his eyes with a small flashlight, and decided that he had suffered a mild concussion.

"Mrs. Barron acts as if she had medical training," said Bob to Elsie Spratt. The Three Investigators were in the ranch-house kitchen with the cook, who sat nervously rubbing her deformed finger.

"Mrs. Barron was in nurse's training when she was a girl," said Elsie. "She does volunteer work one day a week at the hospital in town. Pity she married that old grouch. She'd have made a great nurse."

The boys heard a car in the drive. Jupe got up

and went to the open door. A few minutes before, Charles Barron had driven to the gate to demand that Lieutenant Ferrante notify his superiors at Camp Roberts that a herder had been attacked. Barron was back now, and Mrs. Barron stood in the lane talking with him.

"Well?" she said. "What happened?"

Barron snorted. "That sniveling excuse for an officer has a field telephone, but it's like everything else around here. It isn't working."

"Of course not," said Mrs. Barron happily. "When the rescuers are in our atmosphere, they're able to disrupt our electrical field."

"Ernestine, you don't even know what an electrical field *is!*" cried Charles Barron.

"No, actually, I don't," she said. "But it's terribly important, isn't it? When extra-terrestrial visitors cause the field to stop functioning, everything stops—the radio, telephones, cars, everything!"

"Our car still works," Barron pointed out.

"Perhaps the interference isn't complete," said Mrs. Barron. "When the visitors return, it will be complete."

"And when will that be?" Barron asked, exasperated.

"They will let us know," she replied. She went up the steps into the big house.

Barron said several things under his breath, then followed his wife.

"Good for her!" said Elsie Spratt, who had come to the ranch-house door to stand beside Jupe. "She got the last word for a change!"

Elsie went back to the table and sat down. "That old goat she's married to is enough to drive a saint mad," she said. "If Mrs. Barron says a thing is black, he decides it's white just to spite her. But tonight she's got it all her own way. She's been predicting flying saucers and visitors from outer space all along, and he's insisted that we'll be taken over by Communists or bureaucrats or labor unions, and she turns out to be right!"

"Do you really think she is?" said Jupe. "Do you really think we have visitors from outer space?"

Elsie looked away from him. "What else could it be?" she said. She stood up, suddenly brisk, and got a candle and a tin candlestick from one of the cupboards.

"You can take this with you when you go to bed," she said, handing the candlestick to the boys. Then she went up the stairs carrying a lamp. Mary Sedlack came in and went up, too.

Banales, Detweiler, and Aleman also had

rooms in the ranch house, and they came in soon after. Banales showed Konrad and the boys where they were to sleep in a big bunkroom at the front of the house. Konrad declared that he didn't dare shut his eyes, but he stretched out on a cot and was soon breathing deeply and evenly.

The boys lay in the darkness for a long while after the candle was put out. They listened to the noises made by the old house, and by the people in it. Somewhere nearby someone tossed restlessly in bed. Someone else paced in the darkness.

Jupe awoke in the early hours of the morning and couldn't get back to sleep. His mind kept turning over the events of the previous day. After a time he got up and went to the window. The moon had set, and the ranch was dark and quiet. No one stirred outside. Jupe couldn't guess the hour, but he thought that dawn must be fairly close.

Impulsively, he put on his clothes and moved softly to the cots where his fellow Investigators slept. A light touch brought each of them awake. A few minutes later, all three boys were creeping down the stairs and out of the house. By the faint light of the stars, Jupe led the others past the workers' cottages to the parking area near the sheds. There the boys huddled under a tree.

"What gives?" asked Pete.

Jupe frowned and pulled at his lip, as he always did when he was thinking furiously. "Would it be very difficult for someone to imitate the President's voice?" he finally asked. "And would it be hard to get a recording of the Marine Band playing 'Hail to the Chief'?"

"You think this is a hoax?" asked Bob.

"I don't know. But it makes me think of a famous radio broadcast that I once read about," said Jupe. "It was done by Orson Welles, and if it didn't start out to be a hoax, it sure wound up as one."

Jupe leaned against the trunk of a tree and cleared his throat, as if he were about to give a lecture.

"Way back in the 1930s," he said, "before there was any television, Welles went on radio one Halloween night with a dramatization of a science fiction story by H. G. Wells, the English novelist. The story was called *War of the Worlds*. It was about monsters from Mars who came to invade the earth. At the very beginning of the program, an announcer came on to say that it was only a radio play, but the rest of the program sounded just like a series of emergency news broadcasts. Anyone who tuned in late heard bulletins about the strange objects from outer space that had fallen to earth near a little town in New Jersey. They heard that the strange objects were spaceships, and that terrible creatures with tentacles were emerging from them. Parts of the program were supposed to be coming from mobile units at the scene, and the radio audience heard sirens and crowd noises. There were reports of poisonous gases coming from the New Jersey marshes. And there were bulletins on traffic conditions on the major highways as people supposedly fled from the invaders.

"What the broadcasting company didn't know until the program was over was that people really *were* fleeing from the Martians. Thousands of them thought the reports on the radio were real, and they panicked.

"Now suppose that the broadcast we heard today didn't really come from Washington? Suppose the voice we heard wasn't really the voice of the President? Suppose we were listening to a broadcast that came from around here." Jupe gestured toward the cliffs that surrounded them.

"Okay," said Bob. "There could be a transmitter out there. Maybe it could jam the regular wavelengths by broadcasting noise. Maybe it could broadcast a fake speech. But the soldiers on the road . . ."

"Suppose they're imposters," said Jupe. "That lieutenant is so military—so full of spit and polish. He could be acting a part."

"Maybe he just got his commission," said Bob. "He *is* kind of overdressed. He even wears his gloves nonstop. But I hear that new officers are like that."

"If it's a hoax, somebody's gone to an awful lot of trouble," said Pete. "Why would anyone do that? The fire on the cliffs was—well, it was pretty weird. It can't be easy to make bare rock cliffs look like they're burning. And we did see a spaceship take off. And that sheep herder—his hair was burned! And what about that gadget that Hank Detweiler found on the meadow— that clamp or switch or whatever it was?"

"All very convincing," said Jupe, "but stop and think about it, Pete. Your father works in movie studios. Did anything happen today that couldn't be duplicated by a good special effects man?"

"N-no," said Pete after a second. "I guess not."

"There's only one way to find out for sure,"

said Jupe. "We have to do what we planned in the first place. We have to hike out to the nearest town and see what's happening there."

"That means we go up those cliffs, doesn't it?" said Bob. "Okay. Let's do it."

"Oh, no!" groaned Pete. "Do we have to go back to that meadow? What if someone—or something—is up there?"

"That's what you said last night," Jupe pointed out, "and we didn't find anyone there besides the herder. Quit worrying. We won't go until it starts getting light."

The boys waited impatiently until a faint, flat light began to replace the blackness in the valley. Then they got up and started swiftly toward the meadow. When they had passed the cultivated fields and reached the edge of the pasture, they saw fog. It rose from the reservoir and flowed down over the dam in a fluffy stream. They hiked toward it, taking care to avoid the sheep on the lower meadow, but at the foot of the dam they paused. Each of them felt a thrill of dread. Into the mind of each came the picture of Simon de Luca lying on the ground, his hair singed as if by rocket fire.

The boys groped around the rocks and bushes at the edge of the dam. When they had climbed to the top of the dam, they started to skirt the reservoir. Pete was in the lead, wading through fog.

Suddenly he cried out.

Someone stood in the path—a tall, thin person who seemed to have a head too large for his body. It took a moment for the boys to realize that this person was wearing a suit of glossy white material—a suit that shone even in the dim light—and that the head was covered with a huge helmet. It was a helmet that might have been used by a diver or an astronaut, or perhaps by an alien who could not breathe Earth's air.

Pete shouted again. Jupe saw the creature lift an arm and strike out. At that same instant, something behind Jupe clutched him around the throat. He was lifted up so that he saw the gray sky above and the pale morning stars. Then came an explosion of pain in the back of his neck. He felt himself falling into darkness and then he saw no more.

9

An Invitation to Snoop

Jupe opened his eyes and saw that the sky overhead was blue. The fog was gone and Konrad was kneeling beside him.

"Jupe, are you all right?" Konrad asked anxiously.

Jupe groaned. A pain ran from his right shoulder to his ear. Shaking, he managed to sit up.

Nearby, Rafael Banales was helping Pete get to his feet, and John Aleman talked softly to Bob, who sat on the ground with his knees drawn up to his chin.

"Konrad," said Jupe, "how did you find us?"

Konrad grinned. "It is not hard. I wake up and you are gone. I think if I am Jupiter Jones, I go where there has been excitement. So I wake Mr. Aleman and Mr. Banales and we get Mr. Detweiler and come here."

Jupe looked around. Hank Detweiler was standing behind him, scowling. "What happened?" said Detweiler.

"Someone was waiting here," said Jupe. "I saw a person in a spacesuit. He hit Pete."

"You're kidding!" said Detweiler.

"No, he's not kidding." Pete touched his head and winced. "That guy walloped me a good one."

Jupe touched his neck, remembering how it was. "A second person came up behind me," he said. "He used a sort of choke hold on me and I blacked out."

"There must have been three of them," said Bob. "The one who got me smelled like horses."

"What?" Charles Barron had appeared suddenly on the meadow. "Who smelled like horses? Hank, what's going on here?"

"The boys left the ranch house sometime during the night," Detweiler explained. "They came up here and they were attacked. Pete says it was a guy in a spacesuit. Bob says it was somebody who smelled of horses."

"Nonsense!" said Barron. "Spacemen do not smell like horses. Hank, I came up in one of the trucks. Let's get these boys down to the lower meadow. I'll take them back to the ranch house and Mrs. Barron can see to them there."

Ten minutes later, Jupiter, Pete, and Bob were climbing into their beds in the bunkroom, under orders from Mary Sedlack and Elsie.

"We're having a run of good luck," said Mary dryly. "Simon de Luca could have been killed on that meadow last night, and you might have bought it this morning, but you didn't. Don't push it. Stay away from the meadow. It's not a healthy place right now."

She and Elsie went out and down the stairs.

"She didn't smell of horses just now," said Jupiter, "but she did yesterday afternoon."

"You think she might have been the one who attacked us?" said Bob.

Jupiter shrugged. "Who knows? She's probably strong enough. I think that at least one of our attackers was an earthling. I refuse to believe that an alien from another planet was riding horseback."

Bob stared at the ceiling. "A person who rides horseback? That wouldn't narrow it down much. There's Hank Detweiler. I bet he rides. Barron does, I suppose. Mary spends a lot of time with the horses. Probably Banales and Aleman ride. Then there are the ranch hands who live in the cottages. We know almost nothing about them."

"You know almost nothing about whom?" said

Mrs. Barron. She had come quietly up the stairs, and now she stood in the doorway smiling at the boys.

"My husband is very upset about you," she said. "He told me you were attacked by . . . well, by the rescuers."

"We were attacked by three people, Mrs. Barron," said Jupe. "At least one of them was wearing a spacesuit."

Mrs. Barron sat down on the edge of Jupiter's bed. She had a tiny flashlight and she used it to look into Jupe's eyes. "You're all right," she said softly. "You've been fortunate."

She went on to examine Pete. "What were you doing up on the meadow, anyway?" she wanted to know.

"We were trying to get off the ranch and get to the nearest town," said Jupe. "Mrs. Barron, you seem so sure that we're being visited by people from another planet. Is your interest in the deliverance well known to the people here at Rancho Valverde?"

"I suppose so." Her face was troubled. "I imagine everyone on the ranch knows about it. But . . . but I'm not absolutely sure, you know, that the rescuers were here last night."

"You're not?" said Jupiter.

She shook her head and went to Bob's side.

"That craft on the meadow last night looked exactly like spaceships that have been reported in other parts of the country. Earthlings have spoken to the rescuers. But Simon was *hurt*— and you boys were hurt. The visitors have never hurt anyone before. They're so highly developed intellectually that they're telepathic. I can't believe that they'd resort to striking people. That isn't why they come. They come to help us!"

"Yes, of course," said Jupiter. "Mrs. Barron, the planet Omega is reported to be in the galaxy nearest to Earth, in the constellation of Andromeda. Do you know how far away that is?"

"Oh, about two million light years," she said. "I know. One can't imagine a journey of two million light years. But the rescuers have a more advanced technology than we have on Earth. Distance doesn't matter much to them. They've explored a lot of deep space. It's all explained in Korsakov's book *Parallels*. Korsakov actually visited Omega and he was returned to Earth so that he could prepare the way for the rescuers. In *Parallels* he tells how our wars have been worrisome for the people of Omega, and since we have the atomic bomb—well, there is increased tension in all of the cosmos."

"Um, yes," said Jupiter.

"The rescuers will eventually remove us from the dangers on Earth," said Mrs. Barron. "They won't take all of us, of course, but they will rescue the people who can make the greatest contribution to rebuilding our civilization when the time of chaos is over.

"My husband has always refused to believe that this will happen. But last night after he saw the spaceship, he didn't go to bed. Instead he sat up and read Korsakov's book and the one by Contreras. This morning he is willing to believe that we were visited by rescuers."

"That should please you," said Jupe.

"Not if the rescuers turn out to be ruffians who go about knocking people on the head," she said. "I wish I could be sure they're not."

"You know," said Jupe, "those attackers might not have been aliens at all."

"I know." She smiled sadly. "Somebody could be staging a very elaborate hoax. I mentioned the possibility to my husband this morning and he flew into a rage. I should have known better. He has decided that there are aliens here and he doesn't wish to be contradicted. He believes that they have come to take him away to safety."

"I guess he would like that idea," said Jupe.

"Mrs. Barron, tell me about the staff here."

She looked surprised. "The staff? You *are* an inquisitive boy, aren't you? I feel as if I'm making a report down at police headquarters."

Jupe's wallet lay on a table next to his bed. Without a word he reached for it, took a card out of one of the pockets, and handed the card to Mrs. Barron. It read:

THE THREE INVESTIGATORS
"We Investigate Anything"
? ? ?

First Investigator . . . . . . Jupiter Jones
Second Investigator . . . Peter Crenshaw
Records and Research . . . Bob Andrews

"Investigators!" said Mrs. Barron.

"Solving puzzles is our special interest," said Jupe, "and we are quite good at it. We are not prejudiced, you see, as many adult investigators are. We are willing to concede that the most absurd events can actually take place, and frequently we are proved correct."

"I see," said Mrs. Barron. "Well, perhaps the events that have taken place here are rather absurd, and perhaps we do need some detectives. I think I do, especially. Will you accept me as a client?"

"Certainly," said Jupiter. "You have just retained The Three Investigators. Now tell us about the staff."

"All right." She sat in a small armchair at the foot of Jupe's bed. "We met Hank Detweiler when we visited the Armstrong Ranch in Texas. Charles was impressed with the job he was doing there, and he had the credit bureau in Austin run a check on him. Charles is a great believer in credit ratings. He says if people are careless about money, they'll be slipshod about other things, too. Hank wasn't careless about money, so Charles hired him.

"We found Rafael through the alumni office of the University of California at Davis. He graduated six years ago and went to work for West Coast Citrus, and he had a good record. John Aleman owned his own garage in Indio. He worked on our car when we were passing through and did an excellent job."

"His credit record was satisfactory?" said Jupe.

"It was. Elsie's wasn't so good. She paid her bills late, and several times there wasn't enough money in her bank account to cover her checks. She'd been helping a younger brother, however, so it was understandable that she ran short on cash now and then. She was working as a cook in a small restaurant in Saugus, and with the salary she made there she set her brother up in a little radio shop. She's a very good cook, so Charles decided to take a chance on her."

"What about Mary Sedlack?" said Jupe.

"She used to work in a livery stable in a place called Sunland," said Mrs. Barron. "She heard about Rancho Valverde from a friend who lives in Santa Maria and she applied for a job. She wants to go to school and become a vet, so it's to her advantage to live here and put her salary in the bank. She's never had any credit—never had a charge account or a car loan or anything like that—so there wasn't any credit rating for her, but Mr. Barron checked on her father. He's all right. He works for a savings and loan company."

"And what about the people who live in the cottages on the lane?" asked Jupe.

Mrs. Barron smiled. "They were all employed by Rancho Valverde before my husband bought the property. Some of them were born right here on the ranch. This is their home."

She stood up. "It doesn't seem possible that any of the people who work here could be involved in a hoax," she said. "Look what they could lose. And what would they gain?"

"Mr. Barron is a wealthy man," said Jupe.

"Perhaps there's a plan afoot to rob him."

"Rob him of what?" she demanded. "There's nothing of any great value here. We don't collect expensive things. There isn't even a large amount of cash here. My husband keeps his money in a bank, like everyone else. There's a checking account in the Pacific Coast National Bank in Santa Barbara. There's a safe deposit box there, too. My jewelry is in the box, and I suppose Mr. Barron has other valuables there, too."

"Could there be something else?" said Jupiter. "It might be something you've overlooked —something you wouldn't even think was important, but which someone else could want desperately. Or someone might want to trick your husband out of spite."

"I suppose that's possible," said Mrs. Barron.

"If the appearance of the spaceship is a hoax," said Jupe, "then there is a reason for the hoax, no matter how far-fetched the reason may be."

Mrs. Barron sat thinking for a moment, then said, "I can't imagine what it would be. There simply isn't anything here. You can see for yourself—"

She stopped short, stared at Jupe, then said, "Why of course. You *can* see for yourself!"

"What, Mrs. Barron?" asked Jupe.

"Well, you could see our house," she said. "Everything we have—everything that's personal, that is—is in the house. Except for my jewelry, of course. Now suppose that after lunch, when Maria, who serves our meals, goes to her own house up the lane to have her siesta, and when my husband goes out to ride about the ranch—he does it every day—suppose you come over and we'll go through the house together. Something might occur to you. You might see something that I wouldn't notice."

"A good idea," said Jupe.

"My husband would not approve, of course," said Mrs. Barron.

"I'm sure he wouldn't," said Jupe.

"So we won't say anything about it."

Jupe grinned. "You can trust us, Mrs. Barron," he said.

"Yes. I believe I can."

She went out and Jupe leaned back against his pillow. He began pulling at his lower lip, a sure sign that he was deep in thought. His face was grave.

Pete grinned. "The great Sherlock Jones is thinking so hard that I can smell the wood burning," he said. "Have you reached any conclusions, Sherlock?"

"No," said Jupe. "I'm only considering a

number of bewildering possibilities."

"Which are?" said Bob.

"That someone is trying to isolate Charles Barron completely for some criminal purpose. He is being cut off from all contact with the outside world so that he can be blackmailed or cheated or held for ransom. Then there is the possibility that someone here on the ranch has a grudge against him and simply wants to torment him and hold him up to ridicule. And then there is the third possibility."

"What's that?" asked Pete.

"That our puzzle is intergalactic and we are truly being invaded by people from another world!"

10

Trapped!

The Three Investigators had their lunch at the long table in the ranch-house kitchen, together with Elsie Spratt, Hank Detweiler, and the rest of Charles Barron's staff. It was a silent meal, with each one absorbed in his own thoughts. When the refrigerator suddenly started just as Elsie was serving the soup, Bob jumped as if someone had shot him.

"The electricity on again?" said Pete.

"I've got the generators going," said John Aleman.

"Oh, yeah," said Pete. "I forgot."

Hank Detweiler looked searchingly at Pete. "Don't forget that Mr. Barron's given orders about you boys," he said. "You're to stay off the meadow. We've posted a couple of guards up there to see that you do."

"What does that mean?" said Elsie. "Is Mr.

Barron really that worried about the boys, or is he expecting another visit by the people from outer space?"

"Probably a little of both," said Detweiler. "He figures the flying saucer's got to come back because they left some of their people here somewhere."

"The ones who attacked us?" said Jupiter.

Detweiler scowled. "Not sure I believe one thing that's happened," he announced. "I'd give a sight to know where that guy in the spacesuit could be—him and his friends."

"Maybe they went out over the cliffs," Jupe suggested.

"Could have," said Detweiler, and he let the subject drop.

The meal continued without further conversation. When they had finished, the Three Investigators excused themselves and went out to sit on the back steps. They were there when Charles Barron slammed out of his house and started up the drive toward the stable.

Barron stopped when he saw the boys. "Don't you wander off again," he warned. "If I hear that you've been up to the meadow—or anywhere near it—I'll see that you're locked up."

"Yes, sir," said Jupe.

Barron went on his way, and soon the woman named Maria came out of the big house. She smiled at the boys and walked past them to one of the cottages up the lane.

When Maria was out of sight, Jupe stood and led the way to the front of the big house.

Mrs. Barron was waiting on the veranda. There were a number of cast-iron chairs and tables there, white-painted and formal, looking prickly and uncomfortable with their patterns of twisting vines and leaves. Mrs. Barron had seated herself on one of the chairs. Her hands were folded primly in her lap, but her eyes sparkled with excitement. Jupe guessed that she regarded the inspection of her own house as an adventure.

The boys had decided that morning that only Jupiter would go through the Barron house with Mrs. Barron, and that while Jupe was in the house, Pete and Bob would try to discover what was happening among the soldiers who kept watch on the road.

"I'll see you later," said Jupe to his friends, "and you watch it when you get down near that fence."

"You bet," said Pete.

Jupe went up the front steps of the Barron house. Mrs. Barron rose and went ahead of him

into the hall. When Jupe closed the door, the
two of them stood for a moment, listening to the
grandfather clock that ticked on the stair landing.

"Where do we begin?" said Mrs. Barron.

"This is as good a place as any," said Jupe. He
glanced into the formal parlor with its Turkish
carpets and velvet chairs and settees. He saw
nothing there that any thief could want. He
turned away and went into the music room,
where there was a baby grand piano, a few little
gilt chairs, and some cabinets that held heaps of
sheet music and a few children's drawings.

"My boys did those when they were in grade
school," said Mrs. Barron. "I thought they were
rather good."

"Very nice," said Jupe, privately thinking
they were awful. He put the drawings back into
the cabinet where he had found them and went
on to the dining room. The sideboards there
held some sterling silver.

"Silver is valuable," said Jupe, "but I don't
think your things are worth the trouble of
constructing an elaborate hoax. If a thief took
your flatware, or your silver coffee service, and
then had to fence the things—he wouldn't get
all that much."

"I suppose not," said Mrs. Barron.

In the kitchen there were cupboards crammed with supplies—preserves and jellies that had been put up at the ranch. The labels were dated and none was more than a year old.

When Jupe finished his inspection of the kitchen, he opened the door that led to the basement. Mrs. Barron switched on the light below, and the two went down into a shadowy, dusty place where there was a woodpile and a bin heaped with coal.

"It was just like this in Wisconsin," said Mrs. Barron. She gestured toward the huge old furnace near the coal bin. "Charles wanted it to be the way he remembered it—furnace and all."

Jupe looked around at boxes and crates and trunks that stood on the cement floor. Through an opening in the back wall he saw another flight of stairs leading out of the cellar, directly to the outside. It was the old-fashioned kind of cellar entrance, with a hinged sheet of plywood over the stairwell serving as both a roof and a door.

Then Jupe's eye was caught by an enclosure in one corner of the basement, reaching from floor to ceiling. It was made of heavy metal mesh, and it had a sturdy metal door secured with a padlock. Curious, Jupe crossed the room, peered through the mesh, and saw the stocks of rifles standing on a rack against the wall. There were boxes of ammunition on the floor, and there were explosives, too. A second gun rack on the far wall held shotguns and hand-guns.

"Quite an arsenal," said Jupe. "Was that in the basement in Wisconsin, too?"

Mrs. Barron shook her head, and her face was sad. "It's new," she said. "Charles had it put in about six months ago. He. . . . he felt that the time would come when we would have to protect ourselves."

"I see," said Jupe.

He turned away from the guns and began to open the trunks that stood around. They were all empty, and so were the boxes and the crates.

"Nothing," he said at last.

"No," said Mrs. Barron. "We don't really use the basement much."

The two went up the stairs to the kitchen, and then Mrs. Barron led the way up the back stairs to the second floor.

There were servants' rooms near the stair-way, but they were unused and empty. In the other rooms were huge antique beds with rich brocade spreads. Jupe saw bureaus topped with

marble and mirrors that reached to the ceiling.
Mrs. Barron went into her room and opened
closet doors and bureau drawers.

"There's nothing, really—not even trinkets. I
don't wear much jewelry here at the ranch," she
said. "I just keep a string of pearls and my
engagement ring, and everything else is in the
safe deposit box."

"Is there an attic?" said Jupe. "And what
about pictures? Are any of the pictures here in
the house valuable? And what about papers?
Does Mr. Barron have any documents that
could be the bait for some swindler?"

Mrs. Barron smiled. "Our pictures are family
portraits, but they're not valuable. Except to
Charles, of course. About papers, I wouldn't
really know. I don't understand much about
finance and business. Charles keeps everything
in his office."

Mrs. Barron went out past the front stairs and
Jupe followed her. A small room in the south-
east corner of the house was even stiffer and
more old-fashioned than the ones Jupe had
already seen. It was furnished as an office, with
a roll-top desk, a leather-covered armchair, an
oak swivel chair, and several oak filing cabinets.
There was a fireplace in this room, and over the

mantel there was a steel engraving of a factory building.

"That's a picture of Barron International," said Mrs. Barron, gesturing toward the engraving. "The factory that made the first Barron fortune. I don't come in here often, but . . ."

Mrs. Barron stopped. From the driveway outside someone was calling her name. She went to the side window and threw up the sash.

"Mrs. Barron!" cried a woman who stood in the driveway below. "Please, can you come quick! Nilda Ramirez fell from a tree and her arm is bleeding."

"Be right there!" called Mrs. Barron.

She closed the window again. "You get on with the search," she told Jupe. "I'm sure you don't need me hovering at your elbow. I'll get the first-aid kit and go to see about the little Ramirez girl. Don't be too long. Charles will be back from his ride soon."

"I'll hurry," Jupe promised.

Mrs. Barron went out, and Jupe heard her rummaging in the big bathroom that opened off the front hall. Then she went downstairs and out. Jupe stood at the side window while she went up the lane with the woman who had come to get her. He then looked out the front window, across the lawn to the citrus groves and the other end of the lane. No one was in sight.

Jupe turned away from the window and crossed to the fireplace. He lifted the engraving of Barron International away from the wall, and he smiled.

"Finally!" he said aloud.

There was a safe under the picture. It was an old-fashioned safe and it did not have a combination lock. Instead it could be opened with a key.

Jupe guessed that Mrs. Barron was not aware that the safe was there. He wondered if Barron had found it in some antique store and had had it installed in the house after the place was moved to California. He tugged at the handle. The safe was securely locked, as he had expected. The roll top of the desk was locked, too, and so were the filing cabinets.

Jupe sat down in the armchair and imagined that he was Charles Barron. What would he lock in a safe? And would he carry the key to the safe with him when he went riding? Or would he leave it in the house? Or would he have a second key?

Jupe brightened when this idea occurred to him. Charles Barron was thorough. Surely there was a second key hidden in the house.

Jupe took heart and began to search. He knelt and felt the undersides of the chairs and the desk. He groped along the tops of the two windows and the door. He peered behind the files. At last he lifted the edge of the rug and saw a floorboard that was shorter than the others, and a different color. He pulled at the edge of this board with his fingernails, and the board lifted up. Underneath was a compartment with the keys.

"Not really so clever, Mr. Barron," Jupe murmured. He took the keys—three of them on a ring—and opened the safe.

There were velvet boxes in the safe—jewel boxes. Jupe opened them one after another and gazed in awe at emeralds and diamonds and rubies. There were necklaces and rings and watches and stick pins and bracelets. Most of the pieces were old-fashioned in design. Jupe guessed that they had originally belonged to Mr. Barron's mother.

So Mrs. Barron's jewels were not in a safe deposit box as she believed. Did anyone else— besides Charles Barron—know that? The jewels were certainly worth stealing. But were they worth an elaborate hoax? Jupe thought not. He wondered why the jewels had been moved to the house. Then he realized that this was only

one more sign of Barron's distrust of his own
world. A safe deposit box could only be as safe
as the bank it was in, and Charles Barron did
not believe in banks. He believed in land and
gold.

Jupe locked the safe and turned to the
roll-top desk.

The second key on the ring opened the desk.
The first object Jupe saw when he rolled the top
of the desk back was the metal clamp that had
been found on the meadow that morning. Jupe
turned it over in his hands, then put it aside. He
sat down in the swivel chair and began to go
through the checkbooks that were heaped in
the desk.

There were checkbooks from a number of
banks in several cities—the Prairie Bank of
Milwaukee, the Deseret Trust Company of Salt
Lake City, the Riverside Trust Company of
New York, and the Central Illinois National
Bank of Springfield. Jupe flipped through the
check registers in each of the books and saw that
the last check written on each account was for
the entire balance. Barron had closed out all but
one of his accounts. The one that remained
open was with the Santa Barbara Merchants
Trust. The last entry in the check register for
this account showed that Charles Barron had

more than ten thousand dollars on deposit.

Jupe leaned back in his chair and began to read through that check register, and he almost whistled aloud in astonishment. Millions of dollars had been deposited in the Santa Barbara institution in the past two years, and huge checks had been written on the account. Some of the money had gone to pay for equipment for the ranch. There were checks to a feed company and checks to several oil companies and checks to auto dealers for trucks and to garages for repairs. There were checks to engineering companies for irrigation equipment and to cement companies for sand and gravel and cement. Barron had spent enormous amounts to equip his ranch.

But in addition, huge sums had gone to firms with names that Jupiter did not know. A company called Peterson, Benson, and Hopwith had received money from Barron on more than ten occasions, and the amounts varied from fifty thousand dollars to more than two hundred thousand. Numbers of checks had been written to the Pacific Stamp Exchange, for sums that were stunning.

Jupe put aside the checkbook, frowning. He had seen nothing to indicate that Barron was interested in stamps. And Mrs. Barron had said that she and her husband weren't collectors of any sort.

In addition to the checkbooks, there were papers in the desk—statements from a brokerage firm that had an office on Wilshire Boulevard in Los Angeles. They had sold several million dollars' worth of securities for Barron over a period of eight months. Among the statements there was not a single notification that Barron had purchased any new securities. He had sold and sold and the brokers had forwarded checks to him following each sale.

Jupe put the brokers' statements back where he had found them and began to leaf through another stack of papers. These were invoices and notes, and again they had to do with purchases that Barron had made for the ranch. Jupe was impressed again with the enormous amounts Barron had spent on his fortress. The bill for lawn furniture alone was enough to furnish most homes from attic to cellar.

Jupe smiled at that particular invoice. It was for forty-three cast-iron chairs, Swedish ivy design, ten tables, same design, all to be made to Mr. Barron's specifications as discussed, and to be delivered to Rancho Valverde within ninety days.

It was typical of the millionaire, Jupe supposed, that he had had lawn furniture made to order when he could have purchased it at almost any patio shop. But Charles Barron was used to having things exactly as he wanted them. Perhaps he hadn't liked the designs or the craftsmanship of the furniture in patio shops.

Jupiter put the invoices back in place, closed the roll top, and locked the desk. He sat for a moment, bothered by a small, nagging feeling that he had seen something important. While he was trying to think what it could be that pricked at the edge of his consciousness, he heard a sound below.

Someone had opened the kitchen door and come into the house. Someone was walking across the kitchen. The tread was heavy. It was not Mrs. Barron coming back.

Jupe came to his feet, took one soundless step, and knelt to put the keys into the compartment in the floor. He closed the loose floorboard over the hidden place and pulled the rug over the board.

The footsteps below sounded in the dining room and then in the hall.

Jupe looked around frantically. The footsteps were coming up the front stairs. There was no time for Jupe to get through the hall to the back stairs without being seen. Jupe was trapped!

11

Bob Takes a Chance

After Jupe left them, Bob and Pete hiked down through the citrus groves to the fence that ran along the southern edge of Barron's property. The boys crouched behind the thick hedge of oleanders that grew near the fence and looked out at the road.

A tent had been put up in the wilderness area across the road from the gate of the ranch. Two men in uniform lounged on the ground in front of the tent and sipped something from tin cups. They resolutely ignored the ranch hand who was guarding the gate. He in turn ignored them. He was leaning against a gatepost and holding a rifle. His back was to the boys, who were hiding to the west of the gate.

Pete nudged Bob and pointed to a bulky piece of equipment that hung on a tree near the soldiers' tent.

"What is it?" whispered Bob.

"I'm not sure, but I think it's a field tele-phone," said Pete.

As if to confirm this opinion, there was a tinny, jangling sound. One of the men got up and went to the tree. He took a receiver from a hook and spoke, saying something the boys could not hear.

"How about that!" murmured Bob. "And they told Mr. Barron their telephone wasn't working."

Bob strained to hear the conversation that was going on, but the campsite was too far away. He could catch only an occasional word or two. After a few minutes the soldier hung the receiver back in its place and said something to his companion. They both laughed, then grew silent as they watched one of Barron's men come along from the east, walking between the oleander hedge and the fence.

The man patrolling the fence glanced across the road at the encampment there. He paused to exchange a few words with the man who watched the gate, then he turned and started back the way he had come.

"Hey, we'd better get away from this hedge," said Pete softly. "I bet another man will come along from the west any second now."

The boys retreated to a nearby stand of eucalyptus trees. Sure enough, a second sentry on patrol appeared, approaching the gate from the opposite direction. After he left, a jeep drove slowly past the gate. It was headed west and it did not stop at the camp. The two men in the vehicle ignored Barron's guard, and the guard did not even glance at them.

"The two sides sure aren't talking to one another," said Pete.

"I'd give a lot to know what they're saying to each other over in that camp," said Bob. He looked at the fence in a calculating way, then stared up and down the road.

"I'm going over the fence," he said suddenly.

"Huh?" Pete gaped at his friend in surprise.

"I said I'm going over the fence." Bob pointed. "Look down there. There's a bend in the road so that the guard at the gate won't be able to see me and neither will the soldiers. The sentry on this side should be out of sight by now. And the trees grow close to the fence there, so even if one of Mr. Barron's men is up on the cliffs watching, he won't spot me."

Pete looked doubtful. Bob was the smallest of the Three Investigators, and he was better at research than he was at feats involving physical effort. Pete was the strong, agile one, but he hated taking unnecessary risks.

"If I can cross the road and get into the woods without being seen," Bob said, "I can work my way behind the camp. Then I can come in close enough to hear what those guys are saying."

"Hey, Bob, suppose they catch you spying on them?" said Pete. "They could get rough."

"I'll yell if they do," promised Bob, "and then you get the guard at the gate to come across the road with his rifle and rescue me. I'll get into trouble with Mr. Barron, but I don't suppose he will murder me."

"I'm not so sure about that," said Pete.

"Jupe would spy on the camp if he were here," said Bob. He then darted forward to the oleander hedge and, keeping low so as not to be seen from the gate, ran along behind the bushes.

When he reached the place where several eucalyptus trees crowded close to the fence, Bob stood straight and peered out over the bushes. He could not see the gate or the camp when he looked to the left. When he looked to the right, he saw only the empty road. There were no sentries in sight.

Bob slipped through the oleanders and began

to scale the fence. Once he started to climb, he did not look around. He got over the fence as quickly as he could and jumped to the ground on the far side.

The road was still empty when he trotted across to take cover in the wilderness area. A little way into the scrub growth, he found a dry gully that ran almost parallel to the road. He let himself down into this and began to move silently along on the sandy earth.

After a few minutes he paused and listened. He could hear men talking and he judged that he was almost directly behind the soldiers' camp. He climbed cautiously out of the gully and found himself atop a small, brush-covered hill that rose behind the tent. Lying face down for a moment, he listened.

The voices of the men were still indistinct murmurs. Bob could not make out the words. He lifted himself to his hands and knees and peeked over the tops of manzanita bushes. There was plenty of cover on the hillside, and Bob decided that he could get closer if he was careful not to make a sound.

He felt himself tremble as he started down the hill, but he forced himself to move slowly. Inch by inch he went, creeping, watching where he put his hands and how he moved his legs, careful not to disturb a pebble or cause a twig to snap.

"Old geezers!" said one of the men. The words were clear now, and Bob stopped his painful descent of the hill.

"I get a kick out of it," said the second man. "The bigger they are, the harder they fall."

Bob stretched out behind a clump of sage and tried not to breathe too loudly. He raised his head and looked.

"Gimme that," said one of the men. His voice was suddenly loud.

Bob saw the smaller of the two men reach out and take a flat bottle from the other. He poured something into his tin cup.

"You don't need all of it, Bones," said the larger man. He grabbed the bottle and poured a drink into his own canteen cup. Then he set the bottle on the ground.

The tent flap was pushed back and Lieutenant Ferrante came out into the sunlight. He scowled at the two men.

"Okay, Al," he said. "I thought you weren't going to drink while we're here. You either, Bones."

"What's the harm?" said Al. "There's nothing doing."

"We don't need any boozed-up guys," said

Ferrante. He seized the bottle and hurled it off into the bushes.

"Hey, you didn't need to do that!" cried Bones.

"Yes, I did," said Ferrante. "Suppose the guy on the gate goes back and tells old man Barron you're drinking? How would it look? You're supposed to be soldiers in the United States Army, remember? You're answering the call of duty when your country is in danger."

"Just what I've always wanted to do," said Bones. His voice was heavy with sarcasm. "Save my country!"

"I know it's hard for you—" began Ferrante.

"But it's easy for you," said Bones, "because you've got so much class! Only if you're so smart, why do you need this end-of-the-world caper?"

"I need it for the same reason you need it," said Ferrante, "and we're going to do it my way or not at all. Now shape up or else beat it back to Saugus and stay there. This is a tricky operation. Don't louse it up."

"Why are we going to all this trouble?" demanded Bones. "We've got the muscle. Why don't we just go in there and make old man Barron talk?"

"We've got muscle?" echoed Ferrante. "You

think we've got enough muscle to take on fifty of Barron's ranch hands? And he's got an arsenal in his basement, remember? We wouldn't just be dealing with a bunch of scared lettuce pickers."

"Give them a small cut and they'll change sides so fast it'll make your head spin," said Bones.

"No way," said Ferrante. "I've talked to some of them. Met them in town, accidentally of course, in the Sundown Cafe or the penny arcade. The way they have it figured, so long as Barron keeps this ranch, they've got it made. They don't want anybody to rock their canoe."

"You think they'd fight for him?" Bones demanded.

"If you threaten what they've got, they'll fight," Ferrante declared. "My way's the only way we'll ever get the stuff. The old guy is beginning to buy it, so let's keep cool. He's no dimwit, you know, and he's touchy as a rattlesnake in a rainstorm."

The field telephone jangled again. Ferrante answered it.

"Anything up?" he said. His voice was flat and tense.

He listened, then said, "Okay. Let me know if there's any change."

He replaced the receiver and started toward

the tent. "Barron's on his regular afternoon tour of the ranch," he told his companions. "The hands are working the fields. They're trying to keep everything normal. It's going the way we figured it would."

"Sounds to me like it isn't going at all," said Al.

"Did you expect Barron to act like Chicken Little?" said Ferrante. "He's not the type."

He went into the tent and let the flap fall shut behind him.

"The guy thinks he's Napoleon," said Bones. He leaned back against a rock and closed his eyes. Al didn't answer him, and after a minute or two Bob retreated up the hillside, going even more slowly and carefully than he had when he came down.

A few minutes later Bob was back over the fence in the comparative safety of Barron's land. He found Pete under the trees, looking anxious.

"Did you find out anything?" Pete wanted to know.

"Plenty!" crowed Bob. "They're crooks and they're just about ready to fight one another and let's go find Jupe!"

The two hurried back toward the ranch buildings. When they came out of the citrus groves onto Barron's front lawn, they stopped dead and stared up at the big house.

Jupiter was standing on the roof of the front veranda. He was pressing himself close to the wall of the house and was scowling at a corner window only inches from his elbow. It was an open window; Bob and Pete could see the curtains blowing outward on the breeze. They could also see Jupe's face. It was red with embarrassment—or perhaps with desperation.

"I think we'd better do something," said Pete, "and we'd better do it quick!"

12

Jupe Has a Brainstorm

With a wave to Jupe, Pete began to jog across the lawn to the drive. Bob followed, wondering what Pete had in mind. The taller boy kept moving until the drive took them between the Barron house and the humbler ranch house to a point where Jupe was no longer in sight.

Pete stopped suddenly and turned.

"Do that again and I'll knock your block off!" he shouted at Bob.

Bob froze, his face startled. "Hey!" he said.

"Cut it out!" roared Pete. "You know what you did!"

Pete leaped at Bob and struck him lightly on the arm. "Come on!" he yelled. "Put 'em up!"

"Oh!" said Bob. "Oh yeah!" He darted at Pete, his fists flailing.

"Boys, you stop that!" called Elsie Spratt from the side window of the kitchen. "That's

113

enough! Stop it, you hear me!"

She clattered down the steps of the ranch house and waded into the battle, grabbing Bob by the arm and yanking him away from Pete.

"What's this?" demanded a gruff voice from above.

The boys looked up. Charles Barron was scowling down at them from a side window in the second story of the big house.

"It's nothing, Mr. Barron," said Elsie. "Boys do this sort of thing all the time."

Jupiter walked around the corner of the big house just then. He looked rumpled and soiled, but he was smiling. "Trouble?" he said.

"Not really," said Elsie, and she went back to her kitchen. Barron drew in his head and slammed his window shut. Grinning at one another, the boys walked off behind the big house.

"Thanks for creating a diversion so I could climb down off that roof," said Jupe. He sat down under a eucalyptus tree in the Barrons' backyard and the other boys crouched beside him.

"I was alone in Mr. Barron's office when he came back to the house," Jupe reported. "He started upstairs and there was no place to go except out the window onto the roof. Once I was on the roof I didn't dare climb down. I didn't know exactly where he was, and he might have seen me."

"Did you find out anything?" asked Pete.

"I'm not sure. I have to think about it. What about you? Were you able to learn anything about the soldiers on the road?"

"You bet!" said Pete. "For openers, they lied. The field telephone they have is not out of order. We saw them use it twice. Then Bob went over the fence and got close to the tent. Bob, tell Jupe about that."

"Okay," said Bob. "I heard the second call that came in on the field telephone. That lieutenant asked someone what was new, and they told him that Mr. Barron had just gone on an inspection tour."

"Oho!" said Jupe. "So there *is* a conspiracy against Barron. And someone who works here is in on it!"

"Right," said Bob. "Those guys in the jeep aren't soldiers—none of them. The two who were sitting outside the tent were drinking whiskey, and when the lieutenant called them on it they gave him a lot of backtalk. Soldiers don't talk back to officers, do they?"

Jupe shook his head.

"The lieutenant said if they made any more

trouble they could beat it back to Saugus, and one of them said he didn't see why they were going to so much trouble when they had enough muscle to just walk in and force Mr. Barron to talk."

"That sounds ugly," said Jupe.

"Sure does," Bob agreed. "The lieutenant said Barron has an arsenal here and his ranch hands would be armed and they'd fight for him. Does Barron have an arsenal?"

"Yes, in his basement," said Jupe. "I wonder why the lieutenant thinks the ranch hands would side with Barron."

"Ferrante said he's been feeling some of them out," Bob reported. "Some of them go into town and Ferrante managed to talk with them. He says they like things here just the way they are, and he believes they'd fight to keep them that way."

"Good!" said Jupe. "We can eliminate the ranch hands as suspects. They are what they seem to be—agricultural workers who are permanently settled at Rancho Valverde. They don't want to be disturbed. But there must be a spy here if Ferrante knows about the guns in Barron's cellar. And he knew Barron went out to ride this afternoon. Did Ferrante mention anyone on the staff? Detweiler? Aleman? Banales?"

"What about Elsie Spratt and Mary Sedlack?" said Pete. "It doesn't have to be a man, does it?"

"Ferrante didn't mention any names," said Bob. "I've already told you most of what he said, except that Mr. Barron is beginning to buy it. I guess he meant that Mr. Barron is beginning to believe in the spaceship. He said he didn't want the other guys to louse things up, and he said Mr. Barron was smart, but touchy as a rattlesnake."

"He knew that Charles Barron is beginning to change his attitude toward the supposed aliens from another planet?" said Jupe. "Hmm! The spy is someone close to Barron. And Ferrante and his men are after—they're after—after gold! That's it! I should have known all along!"

"Gold?" Bob looked startled. "What gold?"

"The gold that Charles Barron has hidden here on the ranch," said Jupe smugly.

"You found gold?" said Pete.

"No, I didn't, but I'm sure there's gold here someplace. I found papers showing that Barron has sold millions and millions of dollars' worth of securities. He's closed out his bank accounts in several cities. So far as I can tell, he now has only one account, and huge amounts have gone in and out of it.

"I think if we could call some of the companies that received checks from Barron, we'd find that they deal in gold coins or gold bullion. One of the places is a stamp exchange, and places that sell stamps often sell coins as well. Barron has said that only land and gold are safe investments."

"Why sure!" cried Bob. "It figures! He's sold everything he owned and he's bought gold!"

"Exactly!" said Jupiter. "He's keeping the gold here on the ranch because he doesn't trust banks. He doesn't even keep a safe deposit box in the Santa Barbara bank any longer. Mrs. Barron thought her jewelry was there, but it isn't. It's in a wall safe in Barron's office.

"Now if *we* could figure out that Barron must have gold, so could other people here on the ranch. I'll bet the conspirators are looking for the gold, and they've staged the landing of the flying saucer to somehow make Barron reveal the hiding place."

"Crazy!" said Pete.

"Totally mad," Jupe said, "but it's the only explanation that fits the facts."

"We're going to tell Barron what we know?" Bob asked.

"We'll certainly tell Mrs. Barron," said Jupe. "She is our client. And she's used to dealing with Barron. He might not believe us."

"What next?" asked Bob. "Do we search for the other field telephone? If we can find it, we can find out who's using it."

"Lots of luck," said Pete. "This place is huge. We'd be searching for a needle in a haystack."

Jupe pulled on his lower lip. "We wouldn't have to search the whole ranch," he said. "The spy has to be able to use the field telephone where he or she can't be seen. That means it's almost certainly in a building."

"Yeah, but there are an awful lot of buildings here," Pete objected. "And people are in and out of them all the time."

A door banged, and the boys looked up to see Elsie Spratt coming down her kitchen steps. She was carrying a blue garment over her arm. She smiled when she saw the boys and gestured toward one of the small cottages up the road. "I'm off to see Mrs. Miranda," she said. "She's going to help me shorten my skirt—and we can all hope that the world doesn't end before I have a chance to wear it. There's milk in the refrigerator and there are cookies in the big jar near the stove if you want a snack."

The boys thanked her. After she disappeared

into the Miranda house, Pete looked at his pals and grinned. "I'll bet there's no one in the ranch house right now," he said. "Elsie's getting her skirt fixed and the others are off doing their jobs. What say we take a look around?"

"Okay, but I don't think the ranch house is a safe place to hide a field telephone," said Bob.

"But the house holds clues to the people who live in it," said Jupe, "and one of those people is our spy! Come on, let's go!"

13

A Message from Outer Space

The boys worked quickly, keeping alert for the sound of someone returning to the ranch house. In minutes they had examined Hank Detweiler's room. They saw that Hank possessed a number of trophies, which he had won in calf-roping contests, and also clear title to a Ford pickup truck. There was no evidence that he wrote letters or that he ever received any.

"A loner," Jupe decided, "with little interest in material things and mementos. He's hardly got any personal possessions."

"So he wouldn't even care about gold, right?" said Pete.

Jupe shrugged. "We can't tell for sure. Maybe he hoards his money. Or maybe he just likes to live simply."

The boys went on to John Aleman's room and found a bookcase crammed with books on hydraulic power, on electricity, on engineering, even on aero-dynamics. And under the bed Pete discovered a pile of paperbacks on science and space. Some of the titles were intriguing.

"Here's one called *The Ancient Future*," said Pete, holding up a book. "It's by Korsakov. Didn't he write that other book that Mrs. Barron talks about?"

"*Parallels*," said Jupiter. "Yes, he did."

"Here's more," said Bob, who had opened Aleman's closet and found a carton of paperbacks. He picked them up one by one and read the titles aloud. "*The Crowded Cosmos. The Second Universe.* And *Black Holes and Vanishing Worlds.* And lots more."

"I didn't know it was so busy in outer space," said Pete.

"I didn't know so many people had been there," Bob remarked. "Is it important that Aleman reads this stuff? Do you suppose he's studying, trying to figure out how the Barrons will react to things?

"But that's what really doesn't make sense," Bob went on. "I mean, if the soldiers want to hoodwink Mr. Barron, aren't they going at it the wrong way? Mrs. Barron is the outer-space nut. So why would crooks work so hard to make *him* believe in visitors from another planet?"

"They may know that Barron isn't a man who doubts his own eyes," said Jupe. "They did stage a very convincing takeoff of a flying saucer, and Barron saw it himself."

"Jupe, maybe he's right to believe," said Pete. His voice was suddenly nervous. "Suppose we're the ones who are wrong? Suppose there really is a spaceship?"

"No," said Jupiter. "If there is really a spaceship, why are those imposters camped down on the road?"

"I don't know," said Pete miserably. "I just don't understand. What will anyone get out of faking a spaceship? Mr. Barron's gold? How will a flying saucer help anyone get that?"

"If you were going to leave the Earth and travel to another planet," said Jupe, "what would you take with you?"

"Oh," said Pete. "Yeah. I see. I'd take the thing that was worth most to me. But so far nobody's asked Mr. Barron to pack up his gold and fly away."

"Maybe they're just softening him up," said Bob. He piled the paperback books into the carton again, and decided that the book collection might mean nothing more than that Aleman liked science adventures.

"Just the same," he said, "I'm going to keep an eye on Aleman."

The boys went down the hall to the room occupied by Elsie Spratt.

"Not very neat," said Pete when he opened the door.

"It sure isn't," said Jupiter. He gazed at the wilderness of tubes and bottles and vials, half-read magazines, paperback romances, and slippers left lying on their sides. There was perfume and makeup and hand lotion on the dresser, all jumbled together with bobby pins and a few pink plastic curlers. The dresser drawers were equally messy.

Pete got down on his knees and peered under the bed.

"Does she read science fiction, too?" asked Bob.

"No," said Pete. "Nothing here but dust and a pair of shoes."

Jupe turned to the small table next to the bed. He opened the drawer there and saw more hand lotion and more curlers and a few snapshots.

Carefully, disturbing the other things as little as possible, Jupe picked up the photographs.

There was a Polaroid picture of Elsie at the

beach. There was another of Elsie sitting on the front steps of a frame house. She was smiling and holding a small ragmop of a dog on her lap. There was a larger photograph of Elsie in a satin blouse and a paper hat. She was seated at a table with a bull-necked, dark-haired man. Behind her were balloons and bunting, and a girl with long, sandy hair danced with a slender, bearded young man.

"Looks like a New Year's Eve party," said Bob.

Jupe nodded, replaced the pictures in the drawer, looked into Elsie's crowded closet, then went on to Mary Sedlack's room.

The quarters occupied by the girl who served as veterinarian on the ranch were prim and austere. There were few cosmetics. Clothes were hung precisely in the closet or folded neatly in drawers. The top of the bureau was bare except for the china figure of a galloping horse. There were several books on the care of animals in a bookcase under the window and there was a box of tissues on the bedside table.

"She's crazy about animals, and that's all," Pete declared.

"At least it's all that she allows to show," said Jupiter.

They went on to Banales' room, where they

found lists and schedules for planting and several books on cultivating and harvesting.

"I don't think we're finding out much we didn't already know," said Pete. He and Bob followed Jupe downstairs to the huge living room of the ranch house. This contained shabby sofas and chairs and a collection of dog-eared magazines. The pantry was filled with food. When they went outside and looked under the house, they saw cobwebs and bare earth and beetles and spiders.

"Sometimes searches reveal nothing," said Jupiter. "Very well. So much for that. Now we had better find Mrs. Barron. At least we can tell her that the soldiers are imposters."

The boys went across the drive and up the back steps of the mansion. Jupe rapped at the door. When no one answered, he turned the handle and pulled the door open. "Hello!" he called. "Mrs. Barron?"

He heard the scratchy, raspy noise of static coming from the dining room. An instant after he called, it ceased.

"Who's there?" said a woman's voice.

"Jupiter Jones," said Jupe. "And Pete and Bob."

The Three Investigators went through the kitchen and into the dining room. Mary Sedlack sat there with a portable radio and a tape recorder on the table in front of her. "You want to see Mrs. Barron?" she asked. "She's upstairs. Go through the hall and yell up the stairway. That'll get her."

Jupe nodded at the radio set. "Are you getting anything?" he asked.

"Just static," said Mary. "Mr. Barron asked me to listen in and if anything comes through that makes sense, to put it on tape."

She turned the volume up slightly, and the static blared again. Then suddenly it faded away, to be replaced by a low, humming noise.

"Whoops!" said Mary. "Now what?"

She touched the record switch on the tape machine and the spools of tape began slowly to turn.

"Charles Barron," said a voice—a deep voice that was strangely musical. "Charles Emerson Barron. This is Astro-Voyager Z-12 attempting contact with Charles and Ernestine Barron. Repeat! We are attempting contact with Charles Barron! Please attend, Mr. Barron!"

"Hey!" cried Mary Sedlack. "Hey, it's a message! Hey, you guys, get Mr. Barron! Quick!"

14

Doomsday!

"Repeat," said the voice on the radio. "This is Astro-Voyager Z-12 calling Charles Emerson Barron and Ernestine Hornaday Barron. We are at present in orbit three hundred miles beyond your atmosphere."

Charles Barron and his wife came into the dining room. Barron was frowning, puzzled and also hopeful. He stared at the radio, and after a moment the voice went on.

"Infra-red scanners aboard our patrols have detected tremendous inner stresses in your planet. Before many days there will be an earthquake, with volcanic activity more violent than any we have witnessed before. The Earth will tilt on its axis so that the area now covered by the polar icecaps will move. The Antarctic continent will shift to the equator. The eternal ice will melt so that the seas will rise, and those cities that have not already been leveled by the Earth's upheaval will be inundated by water."

"He's kidding!" cried Mary Sedlack. "Hey, Mrs. Barron, he *is* kidding, isn't he?"

Mrs. Barron didn't answer, and Mary looked at her in sudden fright. "Hey, come on!" she said pleadingly. "Tell me it's some kind of joke."

"The Supreme Council of Omega has chosen to remove certain individuals from the Earth before this devastation occurs," said the voice on the radio. "After the time of chaos has passed, these people can return to be the leaders of a new civilization. Charles and Ernestine Barron are among those to be taken. We attempted a rendezvous last night, but we failed. Tonight we will try again to complete our mission. We will land at 2200 hours to take aboard our own people who are on your planet at this moment. If they have the courage, Charles Barron and his wife should be at the edge of the lake on the Barron land at 2200 hours. They should have with them any belongings they wish to save from destruction. That is all."

The voice stopped and there was silence for a second. Then the blare of static came again from the radio.

Barron reached past Mary Sedlack and

snapped off the radio. Then he pushed the stop switch on the tape recorder. He picked up the recorder and went out of the room, and the boys heard him on the stairs.

"Mrs. Barron, can I talk with you for a second?" said Jupe.

She shook her head. Her face was white. "Not right now," she said. "In a little while." She went out and up the stairs.

Mary Sedlack sat staring at the radio. "Did you hear what he said?" she whispered. "He . . . he sounded so real!"

She pushed back her chair abruptly and bolted away from the table and out through the kitchen. The boys could hear her calling to Elsie Spratt.

Pete looked searchingly at Jupe. "Well?" he said.

"We aren't going to die," said Jupe. "At least not right now."

"You're sure?" said Pete.

"Positive," said Jupe.

"I hope you're right," said Pete, and he and the other two went out into the late afternoon sunshine.

There was no sign of Mary or Elsie on the drive, but a group of men and women were coming up the lane toward the big house. They carried tools and they talked softly to one another as they walked. One young man who looked especially serious and solemn nodded to the boys as he came abreast of them.

"Say, just a minute," said Jupe. He touched the man's sleeve.

"What is it?" said the man.

"I was wondering," said Jupe. "There must be some talk among the people here. What are they saying?"

The man looked after his companions. Several had gone on into their homes, but a few stood in the lane and looked back as if they were waiting for him.

"Some say that the world will end," answered the man nervously. "Some say it will not be the world. It will only be California that will disappear into the ocean and be lost forever."

"What do the people here think of the soldiers on the road—the ones who are camped near the gate?"

"The soldiers are afraid," the man said. "They drink and their officer—he does not make them stop. They do not care about their officer." The man's voice was scornful, but fearful, too. The strange behavior of the soldiers seemed to confirm his belief that something terrible was happening in the world.

"And what about getting out?" asked Jupe. "Does anyone want to walk out of here and get to the nearest town?"

"No. Mr. Barron has spoken with us about this. He says if we wish to go we should try, but he fears there is much trouble in the towns. He thinks that perhaps the trucks do not move so there is not enough food, and when that happens people will fight with one another. What he says is true. If we stay here, at least we have food to eat."

"I see," said Jupiter.

The man moved away and joined his companions. As they went on toward their homes they passed Konrad, who was coming down the lane from the parking area.

"Hey, Jupe!" Konrad called. His broad face was solemn. "I have been in the fields. Hey, that Mr. Barron, he scares everyone really bad."

"I heard," said Jupe.

"I think maybe we should take the truck and go home," said Konrad. "I do not like it here. Here we do not really know what is true and what is not. If we are where there are many people, then we know better."

"Konrad, please don't worry," said Jupe.

The big Bavarian looked hopeful. "You know

something?" he said. "Maybe it is all a trick, what happens here?"

"It *is* a trick," said Jupe. "If I hadn't guessed it before, I would now, after hearing that message from the intergalactic traveler."

"The message?" said Pete. "What about the message? It sounded pretty real to me—if you believe in flying saucers in the first place."

"Lacking in originality, though," said Jupe. "Did you see *The Saturn Syndrome* when it was on television last week? There was an end-of-the-world sequence in it, and when the space-ship came to rescue the scientist and his daughter, it radioed a message."

"Oh, no!" cried Bob. "The same message we just heard?"

"Almost word for word," said Jupe, "including the idea that the world will tilt on its axis and the polar icecaps will melt."

Bob sighed. "Too bad," he said. "And I thought we had something very unusual going on."

"You're crazy!" said Pete with a little shudder. "I sure don't want to be around for the end of the world!"

15

Getting Ready for the End

Pete and Bob sat on their beds in the ranch-house bunkroom and waited. Jupiter had gone back to the Barron house, and Konrad lingered in the kitchen below. He had been warned not to tell the staff that Jupe suspected trickery.

After fifteen minutes Jupe came back to the ranch house. He climbed the stairs slowly, and his face was downcast when he came into the bunkroom.

"Mr. Barron didn't believe you," said Bob.

Jupe sighed. "He says I couldn't possibly remember the dialogue from a movie word for word."

"You told him you have a mind like a tape recorder?" asked Pete.

"I did," said Jupe. "He told me not to be impudent."

"That's the trouble with being kids," Pete

134

declared. "When grownups don't want to listen, they say you're impudent."

Bob said impatiently, "What about the fact that the soldiers are imposters? And your theory about the gold? Did you tell Mr. Barron about that?"

Jupe looked shamefaced. "I didn't get a chance. You know what Mr. Barron is like when he doesn't want to be bothered with something. You can't get a word in."

"Well, what about telling Mrs. Barron?"

"She couldn't get away from Mr. Barron long enough to talk. But at least she believed me about the movie dialogue. She said to come back after supper and tell her the whole story."

"Oh, great," said Bob. "Here we've practically got the mystery solved and we can't even get our client to listen!"

Jupe flushed. He prided himself on making adults pay attention, but this time he'd failed.

"Why can't we go ahead and tell some others about the hoax?" asked Pete. "Everybody on this ranch is a nervous wreck. We could save them a lot of grief."

"But we'd tip off the spy," Jupe pointed out. "And we might put the Barrons in real danger. What if those soldiers decided to come in here and take the gold by force?"

Bob shuddered. "I can see it now. We'd get caught in a shoot-out."

Jupe nodded. "No, we have to wait and convince the Barrons that we know what's going on. It won't be hard to persuade Mrs. Barron. She seems to have a lot of faith in boys. But Mr. Barron might disagree just because she does believe us. As Elsie said, he's contrary."

"Touchy as a rattlesnake in a rainstorm," said Bob. "Elsie has a way with words."

Jupe stared at Bob in silence for an instant. Then he said, "Oh!"

"What's the matter?" asked Bob.

"You said something just now," Jupe answered.

"Yes. I said Elsie has a way with words. She said Mr. Barron is as touchy as a rattlesnake in a rainstorm."

Jupe grinned. "No. What she really said was he's *cozy* as a rattlesnake in a rainstorm! But that's close enough!"

"Boys!" called Elsie. She stood at the foot of the stairs. "Supper! Come on down!"

"Jupe, you're onto something!" said Pete.

"I'll tell you about it later," promised Jupe.

When the boys came into the kitchen, Elsie was serving the soup while Mary Sedlack passed plates of hot biscuits.

"You were there," said Mary to the boys. "Tell them about the message on the radio. They think I've been eating magic mushrooms or something."

Jupe sat down next to Hank Detweiler. John Aleman and Rafael Banales were already seated. Konrad was opposite Detweiler, carefully not looking at him.

"The message was for Mr. and Mrs. Barron," said Jupe. "It was from a spaceship that is now orbiting the Earth."

Pete and Bob sat down, and Elsie put plates of soup in front of them. "If I were you, I wouldn't tell that to any of the ranch hands," she said. "Most of them are scared enough already."

"They aren't children, Elsie," said Hank Detweiler. "They've got a right to know what's going on."

The foreman picked up his spoon, scowled at it, then put it down again. "Mr. Barron made me take the guards off the meadow," he said. "He doesn't want anyone up there."

When no one commented on this, Detweiler went on. "Crazy!" he said. "I just talked to him about taking a bunch of men up over the cliffs into the hills behind the ranch, and he wouldn't hear of it. He doesn't want anyone up there.

Now Mary says that's because the world is going to end and the aliens are coming to take the Barrons away. Well, if we have to go through the end of the world, I think we all deserve a little notice."

"Hank, everybody would panic if they knew about the message on the radio," said Elsie.

"They're in a panic now," said Detweiler. "The only thing that's keeping them from trampling each other is the fact that nobody's running. And nobody's running because there's no place to run to. Why should the people here run when they're already in the last safe place there is?"

Detweiler looked searchingly at Jupe. "Mary says Mr. and Mrs. Barron are supposed to go to the meadow tonight and the spaceship will take them away."

Jupiter nodded. "They're to rendezvous with the rescue ship at 2200 hours tonight. That's at ten o'clock. The spaceship is returning for them and also some people from the planet Omega. I guess those would be the ones who attacked us this morning. Perhaps they're here to keep the people of Rancho Valverde from leaving and carrying the word to the outside world."

Jupe took a spoonful of his soup. "They wouldn't want to be met by a mob when they landed, would they?" he said.

"Just want the Barrons, huh?" said Detweiler.

"No one else was mentioned," said Jupe.

Detweiler snorted. "That's a laugh! Why should they want Barron? He's no genius. He's rich, that's all. Do the rich go first class even on doomsday?"

"It's some kind of a gag," said John Aleman. "Somebody's playing a joke on us. The radios—it isn't such a trick to put radios out of commission, or to broadcast special messages. Elsie, I'll bet if your brother was here he could tell us exactly how it's being done."

Elsie didn't respond to this, but the hand with the deformity went to her throat.

"I'll bet I could do it myself if I had the right equipment," said Aleman.

"Probably you could," said Mary Sedlack, "but if someone's playing a joke, why are they doing it? They've gone to tons of trouble for that joke!"

"Is it possible that Mr. Barron has enemies?" said Rafael Banales. His voice was low and quiet. "He is a rich man and the rich are not always liked. But is it also not possible that a ship has come here from some faraway planet? Could it not happen? The disasters you speak of could happen, too. The climate of Earth has changed in the past. We know that. It could change again. The ice age could come again, or there could be the melting of the polar icecaps. Why not? But even if these things are going to happen, what can we do? Get aboard a spaceship? Even if I could, I don't think I would do it. I don't want to go to some place where the sun is not the same and the sky is not blue and perhaps the grass is not green. I will stay here and take my chances."

"And if nothing happens?" said Detweiler. "If there is no spaceship?"

Banales shrugged. "Then it is indeed a joke—a joke which I do not understand."

The meal went on in silence. The boys ate heartily, but the men only picked at their food. Elsie and Mary ate nothing at all.

After supper the Three Investigators went out and looked up at the Barron house. Immediately a window in the big house went up and Mrs. Barron put her head out.

"Go around to the front of the house," she said softly.

The boys did as she asked. They found Charles Barron sitting on one of the cast-iron chairs on the veranda.

"Good evening, Mr. Barron," said Jupiter.

Barron scowled.

Jupiter went up the steps, followed by his friend. "Mr. Barron, I have a theory about today's events," he said.

"Young man," said Barron, "I thought I made it clear this afternoon that I'm not interested in your theories."

Barron got up and went into the house.

Mrs. Barron came out a moment later and took a chair on the veranda. "I'm sorry," she said. "I guess my husband simply doesn't want to hear the truth. He's planning to leave with the spaceship. He says I must come with him." She looked down at her green sweater and skirt. "He says I'm to go in and change soon. I'm not supposed to wear a skirt to travel to a new planet. Charles believes that slacks would be more appropriate."

Jupiter grinned and sat down. "What about your other preparations? Has Mr. Barron started to gather the things he wants to take with him? What does he want to save when the Earth is destroyed?"

"He says he'll pack his things after dark," said Mrs. Barron.

"I see." Jupiter leaned to one side on his seat and put his arm along the back of the chair. His fingers found a flaw in the metal work. It was a

142 THE MYSTERY OF THE BLAZING CLIFFS

small opening like a slot. He touched it, then turned and looked curiously at it.

"Irritating, isn't it?" said Mrs. Barron when she saw him examining the chair. "All the furniture has holes like that. It's something the ironworkers did when they cast the things."

Jupe nodded. "I see. Mrs. Barron, does your husband realize that what he's doing may be dangerous? He's allowing himself to be manipu-lated. He's seeing events that conspirators want him to see, and he's hearing what they want him to hear. He's doing exactly what the plotters want him to do."

"Jupe, are you so sure there is a plot?" she said.

"I'm positive," said Jupiter. "Actually, Mrs. Barron, we're prisoners here. We wouldn't be allowed to leave if we tried." Bob and Pete nodded in agreement.

"But why?" she cried. "Who are these con-spirators? What do they want?"

"They're the men on the road, and some others," said Jupe, "and they want Mr. Barron's gold."

The front door opened and Charles Barron came out onto the veranda. Mrs. Barron jumped slightly, and he smiled at her.

"Ernestine, my dear, surely you guessed that

I would listen," he said. He sat down near his wife. "You spoke of gold," he said to Jupiter. "Very well. I am now interested in hearing what you have to say."

"Yes, sir," said Jupe. "Mr. Barron, it's common knowledge that you've liquidated all of your assets, that you distrust the financial institutions of this country, and that you believe gold and land are the only good investments. From these facts I deduce that you have put all of your money into gold, and that the gold is concealed here on this ranch. Nothing else would make sense."

"Why, Charles!" said Ernestine Barron. "You have gold here? You never told me."

"There was no need for you to know, my dear," he said.

"The conspirators who want to get the gold have reached the same conclusion I have," said Jupe. "They know the gold is here, but they don't know exactly where it is. They staged the fire on the cliffs and the takeoff of a flying saucer, and of course the radio message from the spaceship, believing that you'll take the gold with you when you go to meet the rescuers. Then they'll have it!"

Charles Barron took a deep breath. "Yes," he said. "I planned to do that. Perfectly ridiculous.

I can't think why I've been so credulous. But only a coward is afraid to admit when he's made a mistake, and I'm not a coward—or a fool." He glowered at the three boys, as if daring them to disagree.

"No sir," said Pete.

Barron shook himself. "Well now, I'll be blasted if I'll let a bunch of green striplings in fake uniforms manipulate me! That young man with the jeep is scarcely old enough to shave. Shouldn't be too much of a problem to deal with him. I have dozens of stout young men of my own, and I have plenty of rifles and ammunition. If we need to, we can drive out of here with guns blazing."

"Yes, you can, sir," said Jupe, "provided all of your people are trustworthy."

"Trustworthy?" said the millionaire. "You don't think they are?"

"Someone on the ranch has been getting information to the men on the road," said Jupe. "Bob can tell you about what he heard this afternoon."

"I climbed the fence when no one was looking," said Bob quickly. "I got near the tent where the men are camped and I heard them talking. They knew you were beginning to believe in visitors from another planet, and the

lieutenant spoke to someone on the field telephone and whoever it was said you were out on
your regular tour of the ranch."

"The field telephone?" Charles Barron snorted. "They said it wasn't working. Why wasn't I
informed of all this sooner?"

"You haven't been very available," Jupe
pointed out. "Now, the conspirators won't let
you walk out or drive out, Mr. Barron—not
until they get what they came for. I'm sure you
want to bring those people to justice, but you
can't do it without proof. And you can't find out
who is the spy on your staff until they make
their move. Mr. Barron, you have to give them
room so they can trap themselves."

"Perhaps," said Barron, "but in the meantime, I'll arm myself."

He got up and went into the house. A few
minutes later he returned to the veranda.

"Someone has gotten into my arsenal," he
said. He kept his voice steady. "There must be
a duplicate key. The lock wasn't broken, but all
the ammunition is gone. We are trapped. We're
prisoners! And there is a traitor! One of the
people I chose for my staff. I have been
mistaken in one of my own people!"

"Yes, sir," said Jupe, "and now we'd better
find out which one it is."

16

The Aliens Return

It was after nine that night when Pete and Konrad stole up the lane and made for the meadows to the north of the ranch house.

"I do not understand," said Konrad. "If it is all a trick, why does Mr. Barron go to the meadow to meet a spaceship? How can he meet a ship when no ship is coming?"

"They tricked Mr. Barron and now he'll trick them," said Pete. "It's all Jupe's idea."

"Jupe has good ideas," Konrad said, "but why does he not come with us?"

"He wants to watch the people at the ranch," said Pete. "He wants to see what they do after Mr. Barron leaves."

"I wish he was with us," said Konrad.

"So do I," Pete confessed. "Never mind. All we have to do is hide on the upper meadow and keep quiet. Then Mr. Barron will get the drop

on the crooks and you and Mrs. Barron will go
out over the cliffs to get help."

"Mrs. Barron will climb up the cliff?" said
Konrad.

"She says she will," Pete told him. "She says
she can do it. I'll bet she can."

Pete held up his hand for silence. They had
reached the edge of the field below the dam.
The moon was up and the grass looked silver
gray in the wan moonlight, but there were deep
shadows under the cliffs. Pete and Konrad kept
to these shadows and worked their way around
the field. Then they climbed past the dam to
the higher meadow.

Fog carpeted the meadow with a thick white
cloud. Pete groped forward until he found a
clump of scrub brush. He and Konrad crept
behind it and settled down to wait.

It seemed hours before there were voices on
the field below the dam. Pete sat forward and
strained to see through the fog. There was a
flash of light and a clatter of stones, and Barron
and his wife climbed over the rocks at the east
end of the dam. The two passed within feet of
the place where Pete and Konrad were hidden.
Pete could see that Barron carried a bulky
package under his arm. Mrs. Barron walked
quietly beside him, and she also carried a

package. Hers was bulkier than Mr. Barron's.

The Barrons paused after they had gone thirty yards into the meadow. They stood still, the fog swirling around them.

"Suppose they don't come," said Mrs. Barron loudly.

"They'll come," said Mr. Barron. "They promised."

Suddenly the meadow was alive with blue-white brilliance. The Barrons started, and Mrs. Barron stepped closer to her husband.

The cliffs were on fire. The flames seemed to shred the fog into bluish wisps and send it whirling on the night air.

Pete heard Konrad gasp. Something round and dark was settling toward the valley. It came from above and it moved as silently as a cloud. For a moment it blocked out the light from the blazing cliffs. Then the flames shone silver on its surface.

"It is the spaceship!" whispered Konrad.

"Shhh!" warned Pete.

The great ship touched the ground, and suddenly the flames on the cliffs dwindled and went out. For a moment nothing moved on the meadow. Then two figures came out of the darkness and the fog. They were clad in gleaming white spacesuits and they wore helmets. The one in front carried a light that looked like a blue torch.

Pete hardly dared to breathe. The aliens paused near the Barrons.

"Charles Barron?" said a voice. "Ernestine Barron?"

"I'm here," said Barron. "My wife is with me."

"Are you ready to leave?" said the spaceman with the light. "Have you brought everything you wish to take with you?"

"I've brought the only thing that can't be replaced," declared Charles Barron. He held his package out toward the astronaut. *"Blight!"* he said.

"What?" said the alien.

"Blight!" Barron repeated the word. "It's the title of the book I'm writing. It's about the flaws in the American economic structure. Perhaps on Omega I'll have a chance to finish it at last."

"Is that all?" said the spaceman. Pete had to hold himself to keep from laughing. The man from Omega had developed a shaky voice.

"That's all I've brought," said Barron. "My wife has her own treasures."

Mrs. Barron stepped forward. "I've brought

the latest pictures of my two sons," she said, "and my wedding dress. I just couldn't leave it behind."

"I see," said the spaceman. "Very well. Come with us."

The aliens retreated the way they had come and the Barrons started after them. Pete stood up, suddenly afraid. The Barrons were no more than indistinct shapes moving through a dream landscape of fog. In a moment they would vanish completely.

But then the aliens stopped. The one who held the torch stepped to one side, and the second one spun around to face the Barrons. His arms were raised stiffly, pointing toward Barron and his wife. Pete realized that this was a stance he had seen thousands of times on television. The spaceman was aiming a gun!

"Okay, Dad!" said the man. "Don't move."

The man with the torch waded through the fog to the great saucer-shaped thing that was moored on the meadow. He bent and fumbled with something, then moved and bent again. Suddenly the cliffs blazed once more and the saucer drifted upward. At first it rose slowly, but then it went more and more rapidly until it disappeared into the night above the cliffs.

The flames died and the meadow was silver in the moonlight again.

Charles Barron spoke. "I presume they will see that display of fireworks at the ranch below—and on the road. My people will believe I am gone, and those pitiful imitation soldiers will now feel free to invade my property."

The man with the gun removed his helmet with one hand. He was quite an ordinary-looking young man with longish dark hair. "You should have brought the loot with you, Pops," he said. "But don't worry. We'll get it in the end."

He moved close to Barron and thrust the gun almost into the millionaire's face. "Of course, we don't want it to take too long," he said. "We've put too much time into the job already. Now don't give us a hard time. If we have to search the whole ranch, we will. But if we do that, believe me, it will be over your dead body!"

Mrs. Barron let out a frightened gasp.

"Be kind to yourself," said the gunman. "Be kind to the lady here. Tell us where you stashed the gold."

Barron sighed. "The existence of my gold

appears to be an ill-kept secret," he said. "Very well. It's pointless to die for money. The gold is under the floor of the basement in the big house."

The gunman stepped back and the second man vanished into the fog. After a moment there was a ringing sound, like the jingle of a defective doorbell.

"Aha!" said Barron. "A field telephone!"

The gunman didn't reply. He stood watching the Barrons, and from the darkness came the voice of the second man.

"He didn't bring it with him," said the second man. "It's buried under the floor in the cellar of his house."

The man with the telephone paused for an instant, then said, "Right."

When the man reappeared, Pete realized that the field telephone must have been hidden behind one of the boulders at the base of the cliffs.

"The gold had better be there," said the gunman to Barron. "If those guys dig up a cellar and don't find it, they're going to put *you* under cement!"

"We shall see," said Barron. He swung around toward his wife and shoved her so that she stumbled away and fell to the ground.

For a split second, the man with the gun turned toward Mrs. Barron. In that split second there was a spurt of flame and the sound of a shot. The gunman screamed and dropped his weapon.

"Don't move!" snapped Charles Barron. His arms were outstretched and he held a gun. "Ernestine," he said, "would you pick up that man's weapon?"

Mrs. Barron already had the gun in her hand. She handed it to her husband as she got to her feet. The man who had threatened Charles Barron sank to his knees. He held his injured hand close to his chest and sobbed.

"Where'd you get that gun?" demanded the man with the torch as Barron searched him for a weapon.

"My father's pistol," said Barron. "I always keep it under my pillow. Your accomplices overlooked it when they looted my arsenal today."

Barron raised his voice. "Pete!" he called. "Konrad!"

"Here, Mr. Barron." Pete started across the meadow with Konrad coming behind him.

"I think these must be the only two here," said Charles Barron. "If there were others, they would have shown themselves by now." He turned to his wife. "Ernestine, are you quite sure you will be able to climb that cliff?"

"As soon as I've bandaged this man's hand," said Mrs. Barron. "You have a clean handkerchief, Charles. May I have it, please?"

Barron sniffed, but he handed over his handkerchief, and Mrs. Barron knelt in the meadow and bandaged the gunman's hand. As soon as she finished, Pete took the torch and went in search of the field telephone. When he found it, he yanked coils of wire from the instrument and bound the two men.

Mrs. Barron took her husband's flashlight and tucked it into her belt. Then she held out her hand to Konrad. "We'll go up over the cliffs and walk out to the highway," she said to him. "I hope you're wearing comfortable shoes. We'll get the police, and my husband and the boys will attend to things here. We won't be back for at least two hours. Shall we go?"

Konrad nodded, and Mrs. Barron began a careful ascent of the cliff. Konrad followed her cautiously in the dim moonlight, moving as she did, putting his feet in the places where she had put hers. Barron and Pete watched the two go up. It seemed to Pete that it was hours before they reached the top of the bluffs and disappeared into the wilderness above the ranch.

"There!" said Barron. "A remarkable woman, my wife!"

Leaving the "spacemen" tied up on the meadow, Barron started toward the lower fields. "Come along, boy!" he said to Pete. "We don't want to stand here all night. I'm sure there's no end of excitement at the house!"

17

The Treasure Hunt

The man who called himself Lieutenant Ferrante stood in the driveway near the ranch house. He pointed a rifle toward the sky and fired.

"Back to your homes!" he shouted. "Step on it! Move! Anybody who's still outside two minutes from now gets his big toe shot off!"

The ranch workers who had come into the lane to stare at the blazing cliffs retreated. The doors of the cottages closed behind them, and locks turned.

Ferrante stamped into the ranch house. The staff was gathered in the kitchen, together with Jupiter and Bob. The man Bob had seen outside the tent—the man named Bones—was there with a rifle. He sat on a straight chair between the table and the door, his gun across his knees and his eyes alert.

Ferrante stared at Elsie Spratt and Mary

156

Sedlack, who sat at the table, hands folded in front of them. Hank Detweiler leaned on the back of Elsie's chair, and Aleman and Banales sat across from the women. They looked angry and tense. Jupe was at the head of the table with Bob beside him.

"Wasn't there a third kid?" said Ferrante. He scowled at Jupe. "Where's your pal?" he demanded.

"I don't know," said Jupe. "He went out a while ago and he hasn't come back."

The lieutenant looked hesitant, as if not certain whether to believe Jupe.

"The kid's not here," said Bones. "Al already looked upstairs. Want me to check the sheds?"

Ferrante made an impatient sound. "No," he said. "It's not important. He can't get far. Just keep them covered." He nodded toward the group at the table. "If the kid shows up, we'll nail him, too."

Ferrante went out. He paused for a moment in the drive to speak to a second armed man who stood guard there. Then he disappeared through the outside entrance to the cellar of the Barron house.

Jupiter Jones looked at his watch. It was almost half past ten. The cliffs had exploded into flames twenty minutes before, and Jupe knew it would not be reasonable to expect help before midnight. It would be a long, nerve-racking wait.

Jupe leaned back in his chair and listened. He heard smashing and thumping from the basement of the big house. Ferrante had come with three other men, in addition to Bones and the guard in the drive, and Jupe knew that the four of them were now hauling crates across the cellar floor and manhandling trunks out of the way. Jupe put up his hand to cover a smile. It would take them a long while to complete their treasure hunt. They would eventually move the woodpile, and in time they would even shovel out the contents of the coal bin and dig up the floor there.

The thumping, scraping sounds ceased, and there was a crashing which Jupe assumed was the cement of the floor being broken with a sledgehammer. It went on relentlessly for five minutes, then for ten. At last it stopped and the staff heard shovels turning the earth.

It was almost an hour since the cliffs had burned.

The man with the rifle shifted in his chair and looked up at the kitchen clock.

The men in the cellar stopped digging in the

ground and began to move the woodpile. Logs hit the remains of the concrete floor and bounced away. Again there came the sound of concrete being broken, and again the scrape of shovels in the earth.

It was an hour and a half since the cliffs had burned.

The men in the cellar attacked the pile of coal. They shoveled and then smashed more concrete and shoveled again.

And it was almost two hours since the cliffs had burned.

Lieutenant Ferrante climbed out of the cellar. His shirt was sweat-stained and dirty and split across the shoulders, and his hair hung down over his eyes. One gloved hand rested on the gun at his belt. He came up the ranch-house steps in a dash.

"They tricked us," he said to Bones. "It isn't there. It never was there. I'm going up to that meadow and old man Barron will talk to me—and talk straight."

"You never take off those gloves, do you, Lieutenant?" said Jupiter. He spoke quietly, but there was a mocking certainty in his voice that made Ferrante look toward him almost in fear.

"It must be rather uncomfortable to wear gloves in this weather," said Jupe, "but it's very important, isn't it?"

Ferrante made a move as if he would leave, but Jupe went on and Ferrante did not leave. He listened.

"Yours is really a most artistic crime," said Jupe. "It required a great deal of imagination. Of course, the raw materials for the plot were already here. You had a woman who believed in friendly space voyagers, and so you constructed a spaceship. You had a man who was preparing for a disaster that would destroy our civilization, and so you fabricated a disaster. You jammed the radios. I imagine you used CB transmitters in the hills around this ranch and you broadcast noise to block the signals from the commercial stations that are usually heard in this area.

"After you jammed the radios, you cut the television cables and telephone wires and power lines. The ranch was then isolated, and the stage was set for the appearance of a company of soldiers."

The man with the rifle stirred nervously. "Hey!" he said. "Time's awasting!"

Ferrante made a move as if to go to the door.

"Are you going to take off your gloves, Lieutenant?" said Jupe.

Ferrante stopped. His eyes went to Jupe's face, searching, calculating.

"You've given a terrific performance," said Jupe. "You were a man frightened almost out of his wits by strange events. You pretended to be a stutterer, terrified of Charles Barron, but bravely resolved to follow orders and not to let anyone off the ranch and out onto the road.

"And wasn't Mr. Barron obliging? He posted sentries along his fence. He warned his employees about going off the ranch. He helped create the climate of fear.

"Then the spaceship took off from the meadow after the cliffs burned, and Simon de Luca, the herder, was found unconscious with his hair singed. The spaceship must have been carefully planned and constructed. A helium-filled balloon stretched over a framework, I imagine. De Luca's appearance on the meadow surprised your men at first, but they decided to take advantage of it. They knocked de Luca out, singed his hair with a cigarette or a match, and left him to be found, supposedly the accidental victim of rocket fire. The illusion was to be completed by the appearance on the meadow of a person in a spacesuit—the one who kept me and my friends from leaving this morning.

"You hoped that Mr. Barron would be convinced that rescuers were coming to take him away, and eventually he was. You hoped that he would try to take his gold with him, and he did not. How disappointing for you!"

The lieutenant was like a statue, a deadly cold statue. His lips were a thin line and his eyes were hard. "Gold?" he said. "What do you know about gold?"

"About as much as you do," said Jupe. "Barron distrusts banks and the government, so he has to trust in gold, and he has to keep his gold here on the ranch. This is his fortress. Anyone could deduce that much. But to know all of the other things about the Barrons—those things that you have found so useful in preparing your drama—you needed a spy. You needed someone on the inside who could study the Barrons and report to you—let you know what was going on. It was someone very close to you, wasn't it, Lieutenant? It was someone who used the same homey expression you used—a rattlesnake in a rainstorm. Someone who has a deformity on her hand, very much like the one you have on yours—except you hide yours by wearing gloves. It was your sister Elsie."

There was a surging, electric quality to the silence in the kitchen. Elsie Spratt leaned forward and glared at Jupe. "I'm going to sue you!" she said.

"No, you won't," said Jupe. "You won't sue anybody. You're going to be too busy trying to defend yourself. Of course, you won't be alone. The lieutenant is so well informed because there's a field telephone on this ranch. It must be very well hidden. Could it be in the stall of that stallion who is so dangerous that only Mary Sedlack can go near him?"

Jupe smiled at Mary. "In time we'll probably find that it was you who suggested to Barron that the radio be monitored," he said, "and not Barron who asked you to listen. It was your radio, wasn't it? And there was a tape recorder hidden in it. The message from the spaceship was on tape, just like the President's message."

Mary's air of competence had deserted her. She seemed almost in tears. "I don't know anything about it," she insisted.

"Yes, you do, Mary," said Jupe. "You and the lieutenant are friends—good friends. Elsie has a picture in her room. It's a picture taken at a New Year's Eve party. There is a dancing couple in the background—a young woman with long, fair hair is dancing with a bearded young man. You cut your hair before you came

here, Mary, or I'd have recognized you instant-
ly. And Lieutenant Ferrante, alias Spratt,
shaved off his beard."

"You want me to shoot this kid?" asked
Bones.

"You shoot Jupe and you've got to shoot
everybody in this room," said Hank Detweiler
grimly. "If you want to be tried for a mass
murder, well . . ." He made a gesture as if to
say that he did not greatly care.

Then he turned to look at Elsie. "You really
are a find," he said. "I should have had my head
examined, getting you the job here."

"What did you expect?" she cried. "Am I
supposed to be grateful for a chance to cook and
scrub and worry about leftovers for the rest of
my life? And watch Jack grow old in that rotten
little shop, making a nickel here and a dime
there? We were meant for better things!"

"Like what?" roared Detweiler. "The wom-
en's prison at Frontera?"

"Don't say that!" wailed Elsie. She stood up,
her face frantic. "We've got to go, Jack," she
said to the lieutenant. "Get out of here. It's late
and . . . and we've got to . . ."

She stopped. There was a distant sound of
cars on the drive.

"Someone's coming!" said Bones.

Jupe looked past Bones and through the side window. He saw a lithe, muscular shape dash from behind a clump of bushes to the big house, grab the cellar door, and slam it shut over the stairwell. The person then sat down on the door and watched as Charles Barron marched from behind a corner of the big house. Barron faced the guard who had been left in the drive.

"Don't try any violence," Barron warned. "My wife will be here at any moment with the police."

Barron had scarcely uttered the words before two cars from the sheriff's department roared up the drive. They stopped with screeching tires just beyond the ranch house. The back door of one car opened and Mrs. Barron leaped out.

"Ernestine, be careful!" cried Charles Barron. "You could be killed doing that!"

"Yes, dear," she said as she ran over to him.

The armed guard by Barron sized up the situation. He dropped his rifle and put up his hands.

There was a thumping at the cellar door and Pete leaped aside. The door flew up and Ferrante's three men started out, then froze where they were at the sight of the cars. The sheriff's men were tumbling out of the vehicles with their guns drawn.

Barron gestured toward the men in the cellar doorway. "They're all tired out from digging for treasure," he told the deputies. "You'll find two more tied up by the dam. And there are a couple more in the ranch-house kitchen, where my young guest Jupiter Jones has been keeping them entertained. I don't think they'll give you any trouble. Jupiter has probably convinced them that it would do them no good."

He began to chuckle. "There may be hope for us yet," he said. "We have some very fine young people today."

18

Mr. Sebastian Asks Some Questions

On a bright afternoon about ten days after they returned to Rocky Beach, the Three Investigators set out on their bikes. They passed the beach community of Malibu, then turned off the Pacific Coast Highway onto the rutted side road called Cypress Canyon Drive.

At the end of the drive lived Mr. Hector Sebastian, a friend of the boys'. They had met him not long ago when they were working on a bank-robbery case. Mr. Sebastian had once been a penniless private detective. A bad injury to his leg had forced him to change careers. Now he was a rich and famous writer, and the only mysteries he solved these days were the ones he dreamed up for his books and movies. But he still took a professional interest in the detective business.

Mr. Sebastian had recently purchased a

ramshackle old building which had formerly been a restaurant named Charlie's Place. He was slowly converting it into a residence. When the boys wheeled into the parking area outside the place, Mr. Sebastian was there, leaning on his cane and contentedly watching an electrician perched atop a ladder. The man was working on the neon tubing that ran around the eaves of the house.

"Hi, boys!" Mr. Sebastian grinned and nodded toward the man on the ladder. "I'm enjoying my new life of comfort and ease," he said. "Once, I'd have been up on the ladder struggling with the wires myself. Today I get to supervise. Actually, I only get to watch. That man is a master electrician, and he doesn't take kindly to supervision."

"Are you having the neon taken off the house, Mr. Sebastian?" asked Bob.

"No," said Mr. Sebastian. "I'm getting it fixed so that it works properly. Then, if I'm expecting company for dinner, I can turn on my neon lights and my guests can find me."

Bob looked startled, and Mr. Sebastian laughed. "I know," he said. "Neon isn't the usual thing to have on a house. But think how handy it will be on a dark night for somebody who doesn't know the neighborhood. Now come on. Let's go inside. When you called this morning, I told Don you were coming. He's been out in the kitchen rattling pans around. I don't know exactly what he's been cooking, but the place smells terrific."

The boys followed Mr. Sebastian up onto the rickety wooden porch of Charlie's Place, then in through a lobby which was rich with the odors of baking. Beyond the lobby was a huge room which had once been the main dining room of the restaurant. The floors there were polished hardwood, and huge plate-glass windows looked out over trees to the ocean. The room was almost bare of furniture, but at one end, in front of a big stone fireplace, there was a low, glass-topped table with several patio chairs beside it. At the other end of the room, partially screened by a bank of tall bookshelves, sat a big desk and a typewriter table. Papers were scattered on the floor around the desk, and there was a sheet of paper in the typewriter.

Mr. Sebastian nodded toward the desk. "I'm having trouble settling down to work here," he said. "I write a hundred words or so, and then I have to go roaming around my estate to make plans for the things I'm going to do here. Like the terrace."

Pete looked around. "What terrace?" he said.

"I'm going to have a terrace right outside these windows," said Mr. Sebastian. "I don't understand why the people who owned Charlie's Place didn't think of it years ago. I'll have a couple of the windows taken out and sliding glass doors put in, and I'll have a concrete terrace running across the front of the building. I can sit out there in the afternoons with a cool drink, and maybe Don can learn to make cocktail snacks."

Mr. Sebastian raised his voice then. "Oh, Don!" he cried. "They're here!"

Almost immediately a smiling Oriental man appeared in the lobby. Hoang Van Don was Mr. Sebastian's Vietnamese houseman, a refugee who was enthusiastically learning American ways. He had plainly gone to great trouble to prepare for the visit of the Three Investigators. He held a tray loaded with food.

"Here is best for good friends," Don said. He set the tray down on the glass-topped table. "Grandma's Graham Cookies," he announced. "Brownies made with Friendly Farms Fudge Mix. Happy Daze Ice Cream and Uncle Hiram Root Beer with nature's sparkle."

"Amazing!" said Mr. Sebastian. "You've outdone yourself!"

Don's grin became even wider, and he

bowed himself out of the room. The others seated themselves around the table.

"I am trying to interest Don in a social club that meets in Malibu the third Tuesday of every month," said Mr. Sebastian. "It's a dinner club for newcomers to the community who want to meet other people. I keep worrying about what will happen to my digestive tract if Don keeps on composing his menus out of things he sees in television commercials. If he met some real live Americans in their homes, he might discover that in this country we do have food that isn't pure sugar—and that isn't pre-mixed, frozen, or preserved in plastic."

Jupiter chuckled and bit into a brownie. He said it tasted fine. Eying Jupe's waistline, Mr. Sebastian guessed the stocky First Investigator wasn't fussy about what he ate.

"Now, boys, what's up?" asked Mr. Sebastian. "You said on the phone you'd been trying to keep someone from being done out of a fortune. I assume you've been on another case."

Bob nodded and handed a large Manila envelope across the table to Mr. Sebastian. "Here are our notes," he said. "We thought you might like to have the inside story on what happened at Rancho Valverde."

"Rancho Valverde?" said Mr. Sebastian. "You

were there? What luck! The newspaper reports were fragmentary. I certainly *would* like to have the inside story."

Mr. Sebastian opened the file folder that he had taken from the envelope, and began to read the notes that Bob had typed up on the mystery of the blazing cliffs. He did not speak again until he had finished. Then he closed the folder and leaned back in his chair. "Good night!" he said. "I'm worn out just reading about that scheme. Surely there could have been a simpler way to go after that gold!"

"Almost anything would have been simpler," said Jupiter. "But Jack Spratt and his friends are frustrated actors, and they couldn't resist the temptation to make a big production."

"I've noticed that myself," said Mr. Sebastian, "in the short time I've been acquainted with Hollywood. Some actors can make a production out of anything."

"And all the elements for grand drama were there," said Jupe. "There was Charles Barron's well-known distrust of the world, and there was Mrs. Barron's belief in the rescuers from another planet. Perhaps Spratt and his friends knew about Orson Welles' broadcast of *War of the Worlds* and were inspired to create a drama about the end of our own world. They must have had a good time dressing up in army uniforms and spacesuits."

"The costumes were from the Western Costume Company," said Pete. "The telephones were army surplus that Jack Spratt and his pals bought. They stole the army jeep."

"We aren't sure where they got the flying saucer," said Bob, "but we think they probably built it. After they released it from the meadow, it floated off and it hasn't come down to earth anyplace. Probably they made that crazy-looking metal thing that was found on the meadow, too. Some experts have looked at it, and they all say it doesn't do anything. It's strictly window dressing. It's pewter, and Mr. Barron is going to use it as a paperweight. We have to guess about some of the stuff because nobody is talking. They all clammed up and started yelling for lawyers the minute the sheriff showed up."

"Naturally," said Mr. Sebastian. He held up the file folder. "There are some gaps in the story," he said. "For instance, the success of the scheme depended on isolating the ranch totally for a few days. How did the crooks keep traffic off the road that ran through the valley?"

"Easy!" said Pete. "They just put up some 'ROAD CLOSED FOR REPAIRS' signs at either end. The road is used so little that they figured no one would bother to investigate. Nobody did."

Mr. Sebastian nodded. "An acceptable risk. Now, who was it that attacked you boys when you tried to cross the meadow and leave the ranch? Had Spratt posted guards there? Was the person who smelled like horses Mary Sedlack?"

"We think so," said Jupe. "We think that Mary saw us leave the house that morning, and that she used the field telephone in the stallion's stall to call the soldiers on the road. Spratt then alerted his men on the cliffs, and they were waiting for us. Mary followed us, we think, to make sure we didn't get off the ranch, and she attacked Bob as two other people attacked Pete and myself. Then she went back to the ranch and took her regular morning shower. That's our assumption, because she didn't smell of horses anymore when Mr. Barron brought us back to the house. I doubt that she knew the odor would be noticeable in the first place. She was around animals so much that she wouldn't think of it herself."

Mr. Sebastian smiled. "Horsey people do tend to have an aroma," he said. "So you found a field telephone in the stable, did you?"

"Yes, we did," said Jupe. "It was rigged so that Mary or Elsie could call out to the road, but no one could call in. Spratt didn't want anyone to hear the ringing the device makes on an incoming call."

"Jack Spratt must be a whiz at fixing things," said Pete. "He rigged the field telephones, and he fixed Elsie's radio with a hidden tape recorder so that she could play the speech that was supposed to be from the White House at a time when everybody would be listening. He fixed Mary Sedlack's radio, too, so she could play a tape of the message from the spaceship. Once Mary convinced Mr. Barron that it would be a good idea to monitor the radio, she just sat in the dining room and waited for an audience, and then she played the message. We turned out to be the audience."

"The radios and the tapes will be hard evidence for the district attorney," said Jupe. "So will the field telephones and the fog machine on the meadow."

"A fog machine?" said Mr. Sebastian.

Jupe nodded. "They had to have fog. The fog hid the equipment at the foot of the cliffs—the tanks of gas and the mechanism that ignited the gas and made the cliffs blaze. The tanks were lowered down the cliffs with ropes, then lifted up again so that no one on the ranch would know that they had ever been there. The flying saucer must have had long lines, too, so that it could be allowed to lift off the meadow, or it could be hauled down and tethered close to the ground."

"The crooks hoped that Mr. Barron would bring his gold when he came to meet the spaceship," said Bob. "They thought they'd just grab it and run. They probably believed Mr. Barron wouldn't make too much fuss about it because he'd feel like such a dunce. Imagine telling the cops how you lugged your gold out to a mountain meadow so you could take it to another world in a flying saucer!"

"It would make poor Barron look like an idiot, wouldn't it?" said Mr. Sebastian. "Well, thanks to you boys, it didn't come to that."

Jupe frowned. "We should have realized sooner what was going on," he said. "I should have noticed sooner that Elsie and the lieutenant were both using the same highly individual expression. Once I noticed that they both talked of rattlesnakes and rainstorms, everything else fell into place. The lieutenant's gloves became significant, and I recalled that it was Elsie who turned on the radio to get the

President's message. It was also Elsie who subtly prompted Mr. Barron to isolate himself. She planted the idea that the ranch was to be a refuge for government officials, and then worried about cooking for a crowd of visitors. Barron picked up the cue and told her that she wouldn't have to, and that he was posting guards to keep strangers out. She was playing on his dislike and distrust of government interference."

"What made you suspect Mary?" asked Mr. Sebastian.

"The message from the flying saucer," said Jupe. "I thought of it while we were in the kitchen and the men were digging up the cellar. If Elsie had been responsible for the fake message from Washington, I knew that Mary might be responsible for the message from outer space. Then I remembered the picture I'd seen in Elsie's room, and I realized that the couple dancing in the picture were Mary and Spratt, and the puzzle was solved. But it was like a jigsaw with too many pieces."

"Complicated, but interesting," said Mr. Sebastian.

"There was a police lieutenant talking on television the other day about confidence games," said Pete. "He said if swindlers worked as hard at something honest as they do at con games, they'd all be rich."

"Probably all too true," said Mr. Sebastian. "I've seen some industrious crooks in my time, but they don't seem able to be honest. Maybe that's why we call them crooks. They aren't straight. Or they just don't see things realistically."

Jupe nodded. "Elsie probably didn't plan to rob Mr. Barron when she first went to work at the ranch, but she and her brother felt that they hadn't been treated right by the world. They thought they should have gotten better breaks, so it would be all right for them to even things out by taking Mr. Barron's treasure."

"Life isn't fair, is it?" said Mr. Sebastian. "We kid ourselves when we expect that it will be. And what about Mary? Why did she get involved?"

Bob shrugged. "All we know is that she needed money for vet school. Maybe she couldn't pass up the chance to get it fast."

"Ambition got the better of her? Could be," said Sebastian. "Now, did you ever find out where the gold was hidden?"

"Mr. Barron won't tell, but we can guess," said Jupe. "The lawn furniture was made to order, and it had slots that were similar to those you find in coin vending machines. I think Mr. Barron bought his gold in the form of coins and dropped the coins through the slots into the hollow places in the furniture. I think his chairs and tables were filled with gold!

"I also think the gold is someplace else by now. Elsie and her brother got too close to the treasure. I'm sure Mr. Barron has taken steps to see that no one else does so again. And perhaps someday he'll regain some trust in banks or ordinary investments. In the meanwhile, Mrs. Barron hasn't lost her faith in the Blue Light Mission. The convention will be held at the ranch this summer, and Mrs. Barron is having a speaker's platform built on the upper meadow. Tanks of butane will be installed there so that the cliffs can blaze on cue whenever she wishes them to."

"Great!" said Mr. Sebastian. "I love it. That makes the neon tubes on my house seem positively restrained!"

"Now there's one thing we need to know," said Jupe.

"What's that?" asked Mr. Sebastian.

"You introduced our last case for us, after Mr. Hitchcock died and couldn't be our sponsor anymore. We thought that if you liked this one, and if you weren't too busy with your own work . . ."

Mr. Sebastian held up a hand. "Say no more. I'll be honored to introduce the case. It's fascinating."

Mr. Sebastian absent-mindedly ate a brownie. "You know," he mused, "that scheme was really foiled by Mrs. Barron's sense of hospitality. If she hadn't asked you to stay for dinner, you'd have been off the ranch by the time the scam started. There's a lesson there."

At that moment, Don put his head in the room to see how the food was.

"Fine, just fine," said Mr. Sebastian. "Keep up the good work, Don. Who knows? Someday you may foil a robbery with a plate of chocolate brownies!"

The Three Investigators

Mystery Series

THE THREE INVESTIGATORS
C R I M E B U S T E R S ™